D1631387

PARALLEL HELLS

PARALLEL HELLS

a collection of stories by

LEON CRAIG

SCEPTRE

First published in Great Britain in 2022 by Sceptre
An imprint of Hodder & Stoughton
An Hachette UK company

1

A CIP catalogue record for this title is available from the British Library

Hardback ISBN 9781529371420
Trade Paperback ISBN 9781529371741
eBook ISBN 9781529371437

Typeset in 13/16pt Monotype Bembo by Barneby Ltd

Printed and bound in Great Britain by Clays Ltd, Elcograf S.p.A.

Hodder & Stoughton policy is to use papers that are natural, renewable
and recyclable products and made from wood grown in sustainable forests.
The logging and manufacturing processes are expected to conform
to the environmental regulations of the country of origin.

Hodder & Stoughton Ltd
Carmelite House
50 Victoria Embankment
London EC4Y 0DZ

www.sceptrebooks.co.uk

For Alice

There are enough of us damned down here! I've done time enough already in their ranks! I know them all. We always recognise each other . . .

– Arthur Rimbaud, *A Season in Hell*
(translated by Paul Schmidt)

Contents

Suckers

The butterflies were beginning to form a paste. They blew across miles of motorway in white and yellow garlands, before joining the carpet of dying eyes staring back at us from the windscreen. Every so often, my father would flick the wiper, and our view of the road would become clear again, frilled by single wings whipping back and forth in the air.

We'd been trapped in our hotel room under thick fever dreams, but today we could finally make our escape. Little pyramids winked and receded in the darkness behind my eyes. The butterflies were not helping. When I tried to look beyond them, all I could see was endless grey underpass and overpass, the road twisting round itself.

'I'm thirsty.' My throat still ached and tickled from the sickness.

'There's some water rolling around in the back.'

I stretched out an arm and caught it. 'Ugh, it's warm. I want a cold drink, like a Coke.'

'I don't know where the next service station is,' my father said, looking at me out the corner of his eye.

On either side of us was nothing but the dark green jungle, roughly hacked back but ten feet high at its edge. Every so often, there would be a car, or several cars, and a police van; drivers and passengers on the sides of the road opening their boots or handing over papers. We were going too fast to tell if they were being searched or just shaken down.

'Can I have some of that water if you don't want it?' he asked.

'Too late, sorry.' I scrunched up the bottle and chucked it into the footwell.

I could see the white bones of my father's knuckles pressing up through the tanned skin of his hands. They were bald from wrist to finger, as he habitually rubbed his crossed thumbs over one another's backs. We had gone to Mexico in order for him to have an adventure, but that hadn't gone to plan. I was up to little enough at home – it was usually possible to winkle money out of someone for a couple of months' fun, but of late I'd had less and less luck. I wound down the window, reaching in my bag for my cigarettes.

'You can't smoke in here.' His stubble looked grey in the glaring light.

'The wind will whip it right out,' I said.

'This is a rental car, there'll be a surcharge.'

'How much is it?' I replied. My father could afford almost anything when he wanted to, but was impossibly stingy about trifling sums.

'I'm not paying for you to smoke.'

'But how much is it?'

He still blamed me for insisting we eat the fried crickets. They came with a dark, chocolatey sauce and tasted like prawns with the shells left on. I didn't see the point in travelling halfway across the world to eat the same food I could find in a chain restaurant. The sickness had come upon us suddenly. We had been in the National Museum, surrounded by obsidian knives and clay statues with hungry smiles. I had looked at the quetzal headdress given to Cortés, gleaming in the low light, stretching wider than the wingspan of the bird itself, and had felt my stomach contract into my lungs.

I wound the window down a little further, lifting the lighter to my lips.

'It stinks up the car . . . We're nearly there.'

The road was straight from now until the coast and we did not turn off for any of the signs to ruined cities my father had so eagerly circled in his guidebook. We arrived in the blue dusk, led up to the hotel by soft light-ed spheres placed in the sand. The bar was closing and there was no food except stale nachos, but they made me a margarita to take to bed. The rooms were all wooden cabanas on stilts, each one flanked with palm trees and ringed with balconies that overlooked both the hotel grounds and the nearby ocean. My father tottered up the ladder and went straight inside to collapse, but I stayed out on the balcony drinking and swatting myself. I hadn't realised we'd be right beside the sea, I heard it murmur-ing and lapping like a great blind mouth. The lime juice was so sharp it made me wince with pleasure. Too tired to read, but wakeful from doing nothing, I watched a little light getting larger and larger, until another one appeared alongside it and they became headlights, before turning again into a single still beam.

A tall man got out from the far side of the car and stood in the full glare as it crept forward. His features were erased by the light. The window wound down just enough for a woman's hand with long and sharply pointed nails to emerge and beckon him over, then it shot out and encircled his wrist to pull him close to the car again, as if to ensure he was listening to her instructions. The man went round to open the boot, slowly pulling out a bulky-looking oblong tightly wrapped in dark cloth, as wide and long as he was himself. He shooed away the porter who had rushed forward to take the other end. Was he really going to climb the ladder carrying that? My trance broke when the car door began to open and the woman stepped out, her smooth white face shining with reflected light, heart-shaped and fine-boned. She paused and turned to stare right at me, pale eyes locking into mine with an expression of amusement and displeasure. I scurried back into the cabana, feeling it enough to be out of her line of vision, like an ostrich or a frightened child. I shut myself up in the silky fortress of the mosquito netting and let my sleep transform the whirring of the fan into giant winged insects just beyond the curtain.

The next morning on the veranda, my father could not cope with the eggs. He'd put a forkful into his mouth, expecting the blandness of home, and had to return to bed, which put paid to any of my plans for the day. As soon as he'd re-ascended, I had them bring me a fresh packet of cigarettes and the magazine rack. The sea dazzled and birds that looked a little like crows were hopping intently among the dunes. A white man with dreadlocks in his beard was playing a little wooden harp while his two tanned babies danced naked before him in the sand. The blue-liveried hotel staff stood at the perimeter, observing him. In the daylight, the tables and chairs on the veranda had a sandblasted look and much of the wooden decking was in need of replacement. It sat between the main lodge and the cabanas like a stage on which the scant events of the day were to be played out for an unseen audience. I'd risen late, like I always did, and the only other visitor stood on the corner of the deck, his back to me. The waiters were trying not to pounce on our plates before we had finished, and talked among themselves in Spanish to fill the time.

<<¡I thought she was a young bride, but she's the daughter!>>

The other tourist was craning to hear what was being said, a fork held half-heartedly to his lips.

<<¡And the pair who arrived last night, I thought he was her son!>>

<<How hilarious>>, I said, and watched them startle.

My grasp of the language wasn't bad, but I seldom used it as I enjoyed catching people on the back foot – they were a lot more generous to you when they weren't sure if you were genuinely annoyed. I raised an eyebrow and pushed my plate away, so as to give them an excuse to leave.

Before the saloon doors to the kitchen had finished swinging shut, I heard them burst out laughing. The other guest turned round and began walking over to me. It was the guy who had refused all offers of help with his luggage the night before. He looked around my age, but had started to get lines in his forehead from squinting too much in sunlight. Unexpectedly full lips for a man.

He said, 'Sorry about that. I get a version of it everywhere we stay.' I watched him navigate the furniture as he came closer to where I was sitting. He moved cautiously for someone of his size, like he might startle and flee at any moment. Despite the heat, his cream linen shirt was buttoned right up to the top and his cuffs were neatly fastened. He smelt of cedar aftershave, with a faintly ferric tang beneath it. I lit a cigarette and blew the smoke towards the ocean, to be carried off on the wind.

'So where is your wife?' I asked.

'Girlfriend. She's resting. Heat doesn't agree with her.'

Relieved that I was not about to be confronted by the object of my nocturnal scrutiny, but also disappointed, I asked him, 'Wasn't Tulum rather a strange choice, then?'

'It was my choice and she said she'd cope with it. Where's your father?'

'Also resting. We've— he's not been well.' The boy was handsome enough that I regretted conjuring any sickbed visions of myself, though I could feel the nausea rising again, probably brought on by the hotel's execrably burnt coffee.

6

'That's a shame. I'm going to walk off my breakfast.' He looked around the table top. 'I notice you don't have a book. If you don't have anything else to do you're welcome to come with me.'

'My book is in the cabana, but I'll come anyway.'

The difficulty with meeting your own countrymen on holiday is they always feel compelled to needle you a bit to find out if they'd associate with you at home. I shucked off both shoes so I could enjoy the sand barefoot. The beach-guards looked at me as if I might start playing the harp as well. In places like this the staff had strict expectations of their guests, they loathed you for deviating from these just as much as they loathed you for fulfilling them. We walked out a long way, past several decades' worth of experimental beach furniture, changing every few paces as the hotels changed. There were entire squadrons of women doing yoga, often watched by the beach crusties, despite the fact there were local women wearing far fewer clothes in the sea behind them. The seaweed lay in piles, almost black and thick as hair ribbons.

We walked to the point where the hotels ended and the rocks began, then paddled out to look closer at a giant lattice of driftwood, which must have washed in from the mangroves. Six pelicans rested on it, staring mutely. My feet were in the surf, arches cushioned by the sand in a way they never were by shoes. I was confused to find the water warm, thinking at first that my fever had returned, and I put out a hand to steady myself against his shoulder. He flinched as I did so and I saw him noticing that I'd noticed, but I decided neither to apologise nor comment.

We began exchanging travel stories. Both of us had been impressed by the cathedral in Mexico City, covered with carved skulls, as if the old beliefs had crept up from the blood-rich soil of the temple below it. He had made it down to Xochimilco, to float among the waterways and observe the flowered boats full of singing families. I asked him if he had done all this alone.

He asked, 'What part of London are you from?'

'Let's not try to work out if we know each other. We probably do.' I found six-degrees-of-separation insufferable at the best of times, I was not going to engage in it here.

'I haven't even told you my name.'

'Then give me a false one, a *nom de soleil*. I hardly see the friends I already have, if we promise never to look each other up it'll be so much easier to stay on good terms.'

He spluttered and then thought for a minute. He had not rolled up his chinos and the seawater was soaking into the hems, slowly creeping up his legs.

'Alexander.'

'That must be your middle name, otherwise you would have said Alex.'

'You can't trace someone by their middle name.'

'So you admit it? I'll tell you mine in exchange.'

We ambled back to the hotel, dodging people selling chakra jewellery as we went. I had believed enough nonsense in my early teens to last a lifetime and was now a confirmed sceptic about everything I couldn't eat, fuck or otherwise put to immediate use. My father was still lying in a fever-fug in our room. He always took a long time to incubate his illnesses and a long time to get over them. He was perfectly lucid, but not as irritable as he might have been. Stretched out there in his striped pyjamas, he looked like a colonial relic and I felt sorry for him. By the time he had the chance to travel, he no longer had the constitution. He claimed to feel sorry for me, because I could not drive, and would be confined to the hotel. I told him there was someone who might be able to help with that. He went back to sleep, satisfied I wouldn't keep on prodding him, trying to hasten his recovery.

The fish at supper was so fresh it was hard to tell whether it was twitching from the citric acid or its recent capture. Everything else was distinctly third rate. 'Alexander' was at his table again. I wanted to say hello and perhaps sit with him for a moment, but his girlfriend was probably still getting ready, so I didn't go over. I was expecting large statement jewellery and a laser-cut black ensemble. The waiters flapped and hovered between the sparsely populated tables like seagulls, watching the holidaymakers intently. I was not eager to be ousted from her place when she arrived, they had had sufficient entertainment for one day. I looked up several times during the meal, but she did not materialise.

He must have felt my eyes on his back, as, finally, he came over, bearing a margarita for me. I tried not to

9

interpret the choice of drink as a pointed reference to my hasty exit the night before. I'd abandoned my drink on the balcony, still one third full, to find it in the morning, seething black with ants.

'She's never hungry, I hope you don't mind.'

He was keen to keep telling me about his girlfriend, as if seeking my approval for the arrangement. She had been his godmother, but had always lived abroad. They'd only met in person this year.

'She used to send us over cases of Tokaji each autumn. My parents loathed the stuff, but I got a taste for it and wrote back one year to thank her. I think I was hoping for a present for my twenty-first, to make up for all the birthdays she'd missed. Instead Oriana came and took me out to dinner on one of her return trips. Then I went to visit her place up in the Carpathian Mountains, it's basically a castle and we just . . . got on really well. She knows so much about life, and my parents say she's hardly aged since she knew them. My mother begged her for her doctor's name, but she told her it was just the result of a good diet. I think that annoyed her more than us going off together. They've decided it's a purely educational trip.' He sounded disapproving of his parents' laxity.

'So they don't know you're involved?'

'It's amazing what people can overlook when they choose to.'

'I'd love to meet Oriana, what a beautiful name.' I had made it a habit to befriend the wealthy, especially those inclined to munificence.

'I know.' Half an expression passed over his face, before he settled it back into a placid mask. Then he asked, 'Want to go see a cenote tomorrow? It's one of the caverns made by . . .'

'I know what a cenote is.' I thought it over for a moment. 'I'll meet you here at noon, if I'm not down before then.'

He bid me goodnight. Before I went in, I picked a place on the empty veranda where I could look at their cabana without seeming to and waited a while, but no one stirred. Even that other world beyond the saloon doors stayed silent. There was only the ocean, whispering to itself. Up in the dimly lit cabana, my father lay still and drawn. He looked worse, not better.

'Alexander' was a better driver than I'd anticipated, a lot of people get reckless when they go abroad. We listened to a Sonic Youth CD he said belonged to her. I praised him for his ability to remain steady even as we reached the dirt roads. We got out of his car into radiant heat; I put up the umbrella I'd brought with me as a parasol. He looked at me and laughed.

'I burn easily.'

'Sorry, next to Oriana, you look tanned.'

There was little point in expecting delicacy from someone who probably spent all his emotional energy trying to make his girlfriend feel young. I decided I could be low-maintenance and returned the parasol to the car. 'Alexander' had mentioned on the first day that she would never let him see her passport, in case he read her date of birth. He seemed continually to be steering me towards a question so absurd I had no intention of asking it.

There was an open carriage waiting on a silver railway track, rigged up to a pair of downy grey donkeys. I went over to pet one, mainly for the opportunity to turn my back on him. I pulled my hand back, its fur was alive with ticks. The men took our pesos and loaded us into the carriage. It was hard to tell if the boredom had made them taciturn or if it was that they mainly spoke Maya. I had read that outside the cities, some people still practised a form of the old religion, but those I'd asked denied any knowledge of it.

We were rushing along the track too quickly for the larger flies to settle on us, and as we went, 'Alexander' took up again the thread of yesterday. He recounted a recent visit to Ek Balam, deep in the jungle. Oriana waited in the car, sleeping coiled under a blanket in the back seat. There a giant ziggurat rose above the canopy, decorated with statues of winged figures. No one now knew if they were shamans, angels, or something else entirely. In the centre of the pyramid was a mouth ringed round with teeth, to represent the jaguar god it had been built to feed. He told me he had stood looking out over the treetops and down to the bottom, wondering how long the fall would seem to one of the sacrifices thrown from the top.

'Longer, certainly, than it must look to those stood by the bottom waiting their turn,' I said.

'Do you think they realised it was vile?' The carriage was cramped and I could smell that he was beginning to sweat under his tightly buttoned shirt. Blue today.

'Probably. But they also thought they were redeeming the price the gods had paid to keep the world going. If you truly believed some things were necessary for the continuation of life, you could do a lot of evil.'

'That sounds about right.' He opened his mouth as if to add something else, then closed it again. He was particularly pretty when he got worked up, that must have provided her with a lot of entertainment.

One of the men led us wordlessly into the brush; apparently, we had arrived at the pool. With the silver track behind us, I could see no indications of human presence in the forest and felt a moment of fear. We kept walking over the dry ground, brushing dark spindly branches out of our faces and swatting away biting insects. It passed not long after I saw the giant crater in the earth. Vines spilled over the lip and out of view, reaching for the water I could hear splashing and surging below. A flimsy rope bridge connected the crater's rim to a steel ladder spiralling down onto a wooden jetty at the heart of the cenote. The man had tactfully retreated. Probably another case of mistaken husband.

Inside the cavern, the light reflected by the eddies shone blue-green and rippled over the white walls, making it look as if the stalactites were still liquid and changing by the second. Most unexpected of all, there were bats towards the back of the cave, swooping over the water. They had made their homes in the rock.

I exclaimed, 'We're inside a fallen star!'

I was used to intriguing boys by seeming older than I was, but now I had to play the ingénue, for the sake of contrast. It was very tiresome trying to shape myself around someone I had only caught a glimpse of. If I succeeded in charming him enough, perhaps she might be enticed out of the room.

He asked, 'Can I tell you something?'

'Depends on what it is.'

He had a guilty, furtive expression. 'Have you noticed anything unusual . . . about what I've told you of Oriana's . . . condition?'

I put on my most innocent voice. 'Why, should I have done?'

'Don't make me say it.'

I laughed at him. He looked so shocked and annoyed that I found myself doubled over for a good few minutes, laughter echoing from the rocks around us.

'You can't be serious.'

'I am.' He looked me square in the face and lifted a hand to his neck to touch the space between his collar-bone and his jugular. 'She's going to change me soon.' He seemed proud of this fact.

'You know I don't believe you, right? No one sane could.' I held a hand over my chest as if I could force the hilarity back in.

'There is no evidence I would be permitted to show you that's worth seeing. Besides, it doesn't matter to me whether you believe me or not, in fact it's better that you don't.'

I started to undress. 'I don't, but I'll behave like I do, since we're on holiday. You seem harmless enough for a lunatic.'

'Thank you.'

He eventually followed suit, leaving his clothes by mine on the jetty and slipping into the cool, clear water. Striations laced along his forearms, hips and neck, some newer and pinker than others. I wanted to trace the marks she had made on him, to feel the patterns of her thought. Instead, I pointed at a web of them, but didn't quite make contact.

'Do you . . . like . . . it?'

'Sometimes.'

At least he had a better idea than most men ever will of what it is like to be owned by someone else. I began to wonder about her long-term plans for him, she couldn't string this out indefinitely.

The circle of sunlight above us was blinding. I doubted that Oriana was shrinking from the same light, back in the hotel. She was probably having lunch on the deck and laughing at the con she had pulled off. I envied her the sheer daring. No doubt he'd hoped I would urge him to run away, to get out before it was too late, before she did something to him that he could not hope to heal from. There was something delicious about his credulity and the knowledge I wouldn't do anything to help him.

I had neglected to eat anything before our excursion, not knowing what activities it might entail. During the car ride back to the hotel, I counted crimson flame trees to distract myself from the contortions of my gut. As I was washing the residue of the day off my overheated skin, I was annoyed to feel a rush of pity for 'Alexander' in his too-neat chinos and sunbleached hair, kitted out in Oriana's fantasy. Of course she had brought him here, surely no one could be prevailed upon to indulge such silliness in Europe. I doubled over and gasped, then rolled my eyes, thinking this must be some poorly repressed emotion. Then I started vomiting bile, clear and acrid. When it stopped for long enough, I forced on the clothes I could find on the floor and dragged myself into the bed. I would have a short siesta. I was supposed to meet him again after sunset.

Several times, I'm not sure how many, I managed to get out of bed to go and prepare myself. Each effort sent me running back to the bathroom or the bed. I was not even capable of closing the door to the balcony. None of this was made easier by the need to attempt creeping through the room, as my father lay looking pained in the other bed. Eventually I would simply lift my head and feel determined, while already falling back into the fever dream. Sandfeel. The pelicans scoring their own breasts with their beaks, lattice vibrating with the music as they played themselves like gory violins. I could feel the vibrations in the sands. The warm sands hardening into a shining black blade. Her white hand held it as she scored the earth, drawing more dark blood from the soil.

Enough to feed a diving god or a jaguar. The jaguar that stalked the room would feed on him instead of me, I would be spared another cycle. The light reflected from its black fur. The sands glimmered, refracted into little insects. I was being fed on by the insects, I must draw down the netting.

I sat bolt upright.

The figure silhouetted against the open door drew itself up and turned to me. It was too short to be 'Alexander'. I could not see a face, but her long nails were black spokes against the moonlight. I waited for my eyes to adjust but there was only deeper darkness. I held what I thought must be her gaze and slowly pulled the white netting away from me like a bride. We waited like that until the little holes of the canopy fizzled back into the static of my dream.

In flashes I watched the figure creep closer, step by step, until the afternoon of the next day, when at last I reached out for water and touched the lamp instead to ensure that it, at least, was real. She had not reached me, but I felt a pang to have missed the moment when she turned away.

I tried to eat some crumbly salted crackers I'd found in a suitcase. My throat was still raw and tight, but I managed. A note from 'Alexander' had been put under the door to the cabana stairs, expressing the hope I would be able to join him that evening. They would be leaving soon. I washed the fever from my hair with a cold shower and told myself to get a grip. They could go on to play their games at the next resort, with the next bored traveller they came across, but there was still time enough for me to play my own.

That evening, we cradled huge balloon glasses of cognac and sat in a rattan orb that had been left on the beach. He was attentive, but seemed to sense my embarrassment and did not bring up my sickness more than was necessary. In return, I did not mention the delusions his strange confession had provoked in me. He'd brought a heavy blanket from their room. The side we were sitting under was wool, and the other was dark fur, short and rather coarse. It smelt faintly of some unidentified creature. If I had known anything about astronomy, the constellations would probably have looked foreign to me. Rather than ask about them I chose to toy with him instead.

'If you are telling the truth, I don't suppose there's any chance you'd take me with you?' I didn't really want this of course, to be in the thrall of this woman forever like 'Alexander', and besides I had my father to take me on holidays and drive me everywhere.

'She would never agree to it, it takes so much out of her even to help me. Besides, I've had to leave behind everyone I've ever known. You have your father.'

I pressed. 'I think he'd get over it. My siblings are far more accomplished.'

18

'The two of us? It would look like we'd run off to-gether. One death is a tragic accident, or at least it would be if my parents cared.'

'You came here to disappear, didn't you?'

'It would be too complicated to maintain a lie. I will be in no state to leave the house during their life-times. It's a good thing I won't know how to find you, for your own safety.' He looked out at the sea, towards the floating driftwood. 'She said she'll tell them that I drowned.'

His mouth did have the cast I imagined a man might wear when he is resolved to cut off the foot that keeps him in a trap, because otherwise he will starve to death. His certainty was such that for a moment I almost be-lieved it too. I touched a curl of hair that had fallen down over his forehead, very gently. He was in so much danger, yet he thought he was soon to be free.

'You know, you might as well. Since you won't have any self-control for such a long time after.'

'I would – but I'd like to remember myself as exercising that self-control, I think. I'll take a kiss as proof of that.'

I felt my youth seething in my veins, the only one I'd ever have. At least I knew that.

'What you mean is you'll enjoy remembering the girl you turned down on the beach from time-to-time, when I'm just a hank of hair and some yellow bones, in among all the other anonymous dead.'

'You sound like you'd prefer my version of you too.'

'I suppose, though, I'll still be anonymous to you.'

'How does it go? I used to know this by heart when I was at school "The love where Death has set his seal/ Nor age can chill, nor rival steal,/ Nor falsehood disavow . . ."'

'The *falsehood*, as you put it, is yours, but I'll kiss you anyway, you pretentious bastard.'

I wanted her to see us then, out of the window of her cabana. She might have filled his mind with lies, but I could still enjoy his body if I chose. Anticipating the consequences he would suffer at her hands for his infidelity brought more pleasure than the act itself. I would not be the last to touch him, but I would be the one to damn him, after all.

In the early hours, I was awakened by a loud click. My father's snoring continued unabated. I went to check the door to the balcony but it was locked, I'd made certain of that after parting from 'Alexander'. Headlights shone brightly through the wooden slats and I crept outside to see what was happening. Oriana stood illuminated, tapping her foot, one hand on the car boot she had just closed. She stood quite alone, no men to help her and no need of them. Before she slid into the driver's seat to set off, she looked up at me and grinned crimson.

My father had recovered enough the next morning to sit with me at breakfast, poking the eggs cautiously. He was asking about my new friend and when he would get to meet this nice young man. It was then the waiters rushed onto the beach and lifted his body from the surf.

Unfinished and Unformed

Emet. Met. Emet. Met. Light. Dark. Light. Dark.

In the beginning, these were the only distinctions. Then came sound and silence, movement and stillness.

I had limbs and those limbs were moving. I chopped the wood and brought it in, then I swept the floors. I had hands, I used my hands to stir the pot and scrub it when it was empty. I had fingers, I held a grey-white bone-handled knife between them to cut up cabbages and onions.

The woman cut the chickens herself, brought them near to the door, hanging by the legs, shrieking and flapping. She stilled them with the little knife. The blood was collected in a scratched tin pan at her feet, where it was joined by glossy feathers, their brightness slowly dulling as they sank. She cut out the major veins and threw them on top of the mess. They looked like purple worms the chickens themselves would have pecked excitedly from the ground. They leaked more blood onto the feathers, I could smell it. It was like the head of the axe I used to cut trees in the forest. But I didn't want to put the axe head in my mouth.

She seemed to think that when she rubbed the aleph from the wax tablet which hung around my neck that I would be still the way the chickens were still. I felt her pick me up and put me in the corner of the room, under a blanket. I could hear the hiss of the broth as the pot kept boiling on the embers of the fire, the birds singing in the trees outside, the stream running past at the edge of the plot we lived on.

She sang in another language I did not yet know, familiar but alien. She spoke in it as well, I could not see if she was reading or reciting. I could smell her eating the food we had made. She would rub off the aleph before sundown one day and scratch it back on some time after sundown the next. As the days separated out and I began to understand the routines by which we lived, it became clearer that this happened once a week.

Plum trees grew on the plot, dark plums with a silvery-blue fur that was easily scraped off, like the powder from a butterfly's wing. She made me go out with a little stepladder and a woven basket to gather them before they fell. Instead of eating these, she would put them into large clay pots in the cellar and leave them until they produced a sweet, musty smell, not unlike the plaited bread she baked after I had finished kneading dough. She would go to the cellar sometimes and poke at these pots with a stick to check on them. Nearby was a store of bottles containing a clear liquid that burnt my mouth and also smelt faintly of plums. Sometimes when I was dead, she would drink lots of this liquid and cradle me on her lap, rocking me back and forth. Her hands were rough from the work she did before she made me, but still felt small and plump. Because she did not know that

I could think, she never guessed these were the times that I liked best.

She told me that her father was a very wise man, who lived over the mountains to the west. When he sang his holy songs, the animals would stand on their hind legs to listen. Even the szlachta respected him, and, it was said, sent emissaries to hear his advice. He was so pure that the spirits of righteous men who still had tasks to complete on Earth could occupy his body for a time to use it. I wanted to ask if I was a righteous man, to be living in my shell of clay, but I did not have the gift of speech, alive or dead. Her father had taught her how to read and write and had chosen not to notice when she read books intended only for learned men. Ancient books and new ones, from as far away as Prague.

She told me the story of how she had met her Hiram, with his glossy black curls and broad shoulders. He would come to the window of the kitchen to sell ribbons and lace and other things. The servant girl would try to shoo him away, but she was almost as reluctant as her mistress to see him go. He wandered through all the shtetls, tracing his route back and forth. Increasingly, he traced it back to her, sung new songs to her that nobody who lived nearby had sung her yet. She was promised to a second cousin, kind and also very learned, but the pedlar was the only man who interested her. It became clear she had been too interested in him. Her father married them himself, with two of the poorest men in the settlement as witnesses, and recited the story of Jacob's flight from the house of Laban. There was no dancing that day.

Despite these Sabbath intimacies, she didn't like me much when I was alive. If I dawdled bringing back the logs, or let the stew burn in the pot, she would smack the back of my head. It was neither pleasant nor unpleasant, simply a feeling of sudden pressure. No matter how hard she hit, my head would slowly swell back out, erasing the impression of her hand. Once, she said to me:

'Be more careful, you ugly golem! Without a soul, you cannot speak. If you cannot speak, you can't ask questions. So listen when I talk!'

I had not known that I was ugly. I'd imagined that I must look like a clay copy of her, with dark brown eyes and a pointed chin. Perhaps she thought that she was ugly? The next time her clothes were dirty, I went to wash them in the shallow pool nearby. I hadn't thought to study myself before. I was grey and lumpen, with a wide slashed mouth and broad, crude nose. She'd never meant for me to be looked at. I remembered her face and marked the points of difference. Yet as I watched my reflection flickering on the water, it slowly came to look more and more like her, until I was standing in her image, quite naked on the bank. I wrung out a wet dress and put it on, tucking the wax tablet out of sight. I was beautiful.

Just then, Nama the basket weaver's wife, who lived on the neighbouring plot, came with her own clothes to wash. I'd never seen Nama, though I'd heard her through the blankets that covered my hiding place, when she came round to talk about the settlement. She gave information not as if she wished to share it with my Creator, but as if she were unloading part of some heavy burden every time she visited.

'You shouldn't come out here alone. Look at yourself, you're all soaked. When is that husband of yours going to return? Mine came back from town yesterday and they're all saying there's going to be another revolt. The szlachta told our collectors to ask for higher rents. Isaac can keep me safe, but what will you do, all alone in that house?'

I stared at her, the hair shoved back under a patterned scarf, the breasts pulling in opposite directions. She too had a dark patch beneath each eye. I wasn't sure my new form would hold and had no practice making expressions with my Creator's face.

'Do you have anything to tell me?'

I moved my new lips, but still could not reply.

'Not a word of thanks! You always were a proud woman. Well, don't expect another warning from me!'

She picked up her heap of clothes and went in search of a different washing spot.

My face in the water changed again, first to the new face that I'd just learnt, then to my original ugliness. Every time I came out to the pool, I did it again. For variety, I also tried to change my face to look like one of the chickens, but that never succeeded. My Creator didn't like to send me so far out of her sight, fearing that I would be discovered. My encounter with Nama must have occurred because she'd believed Nama to be elsewhere. There was soon more work to do than ever: the wall-carpets that kept some of the cold out of the little house at night had to be beaten, the floor scrubbed, fruits and berries had to be boiled down into preserves and vegetables pickled in salt water.

She did not like to venture into the shtetl, she said they all knew who she'd been and what she'd done. No man whose life is taken up with the written word could understand how the talk of women travels so far without it. But she had to go and sell her pots of musty plums to the tavern keeper to be transformed into liquor. There were always other things she had to buy because she couldn't make them, even though she had made life itself. As I was sweeping the floor, a brown beetle ran ahead of my broom. I snatched it up and turned my hand so it lay curled in the valley of my palm. Gradually, it stretched out its legs, as fine as hairs, and ran up my fingers, climbing as I turned my hand. I shook it off onto the table and spent the afternoon making it run to and fro, blocking its path and guiding it in smaller and larger circles. I did not realise it was nearly sunset until she was standing over me. She crushed the beetle with her fist and hauled me to my feet.

'Hiram is coming tomorrow night and you have wasted the whole day. You are not a child, you were made to work. Get on with it, or I'll return you to the dust!'

So, for the first time, I watched her doing her Sabbath observances, carefully ignoring me as I finished all my tasks. At nightfall the next day she bundled me in two shawls and pushed me out of sight. When Hiram finally returned, she asked him, 'Did you see him? Did you see our son? Is he well?'

And even though Hiram told her no, his grandfather had again insisted that the boy's studies would be disrupted and he could not come outside, it was then that I first knew rage. She had made someone else before me, and cared for him, even though she couldn't see him.

For the next week I lay there listening, they barely left the house. She was Hiram's flower, his jewel, he still adored her. She fed him all the delicacies we had made.

He said he was sorry she had to work so hard for so little gain, that fewer people seemed to want his wares each time he passed through the settlements. Last year's harvest had been bad, so times were bad for everyone. She accused him of having another wife, another family, but I did not hear any sound of slapping, and her voice sounded different than it did when she reprimanded me. It was only after they'd finished laughing that I understood how seldom she had laughed before.

I grew bolder when he was gone. He had left behind a dark mirror in a carved wooden frame, which nobody would buy because it had a fracture-line in the corner. Whenever my Creator was out of the house, I would sit at the table on the chair and run through her expressions in the glass. I could smile, raise an eyebrow, frown and grimace. Tears were beyond me. I liked to mouth words and pretend that I was speaking.

One morning, she went into the woods to gather mushrooms, saying I could not be trusted to choose safely.

I ventured to put on her least torn dress and sat brushing out hair that was not mine, admiring eyes that were not mine either. If I had this face, Hiram would love me.

A shout came from the woods, then the sound of something big falling. She ran through the door with leaves and grasses in her hair, so fast that the sight of me only stopped her halfway to the cellar. She grabbed my elbow, as if about to strike me for my insolence in imitating her, then looked back at the open door behind us. She threw me halfway across the room towards it and bolted. As I heard the trapdoor in the corner snick closed, I found myself lying on the floor, looking at two brown leather boots thick with filth.

The man had a large, round beard and wore a long loose-belted coat. He was talking very fast, and some of his words were the same words the woman used, but I could not understand him. He picked me up and sat on the bed with me resting on his lap, the way she sometimes held me. The man unbelted his coat and pulled a little flask from the inside pocket, offering it to me before taking a swig from it. He was still talking, but more slowly now. Without warning, he yanked up my dress to the level of my neck, to put his large hairy hands on my breasts. I was off his lap now and lying on the bed as he let his britches drop. He was breathing in the same way Hiram breathed during his visit. Maybe this was what men did. He seemed to be searching for something on my body, though as far as I could tell, I had made myself look like her in every particular.

She was coming out of the cellar now, silently behind him.

The prodding continued, the man was getting more and more annoyed. I knew that the bed should be moving at this point, so I curled my legs around him and hurled myself back a few times. Was that it? He grabbed both my shoulders and pushed harder.

She drew the little knife across his throat.

The blood was in my eyes and mouth and on my tongue. When that ran out, I put my lips up to the wound and licking became eating. I crunched the bones and sucked the marrow. I savoured the brain and swallowed the organs, slippery and rich. There was not much left of him now but skin shreds. She still held the knife, with an expression of disgust.

She snatched the tablet from around my neck and clutched it in her other hand as if she wished to break it. She looked down at the man's big leather boots and sighed. Taking the knife, she scored along the edges of the wax on each side of the tablet, levering from their frames the emet and the tetragrammaton. She took my chin in her bloodied hand and put the words inside my mouth.

These were sweet and bitter going down. Now I knew the difference between pain and pleasure. I knew that I could name myself and one day I could die.

'If Adonai sees fit to give you a soul, perhaps you will understand what it is you've done.'

I thanked her and went to put on the Cossack's clothes, after I'd put on his face.

raw pork and opium

Between the two Christmases, we spent most of our time at Dima's ruined mansion. We had begun using the Orthodox calendar to find excuses for parties, having exhausted our Gregorian options. The mansion was comprised of two conjoined houses knocked through to form a labyrinthine whole, with two staircases back-to-back, splaying out into long corridors and sudden attics. There was a hole in the roof over one of the stairwells and the little ballroom was full of dead leaves. Dima lived alone there with his space heater, mourning the fact he was too old to be a musical prodigy.

We were accustomed to checking in and checking out of the continuous party as we chose. Frequently, we would become lost and fall asleep in out-of-the-way rooms. Dima would grumble to himself, though he never sent us home. We liked to say that the house had its favourites too. Jackets, purses and martini glasses gungy with our lipstick would abruptly disappear and re-emerge days later. The house belonged to family friends in Uzbekistan, for whom he was minding it indefinitely. Every so often they would think about selling it and Dima would panic at the prospect of finding regular work, but they always lost interest after a few weeks of men in shiny suits coming round to disapprove of the decay.

It was crisp and dark inside the house and out. We had brought large quantities of candles. As bottles multiplied, the old ballroom slowly became illuminated, at least until the next draught came through. An abandoned canvas depicting Carly's attempt to copy Bouguereau's *Dante and Virgil* had been pinned over the most broken window, but several others sported worrying fractures. Dima wandered round in his patterned dressing gown, checking on guests scattered throughout the house. Even he would sometimes become disorientated and put his head back round the door, thinking he was looking into a different room. He'd recently discovered some of the doorknobs had been made by Lalique and was now convinced a particularly cultured thief might know this too and take them. We were becoming convinced that the guests we didn't know were the same guests who had been in the background of most of the parties we had ever been to. Perhaps we were always in the background of theirs.

One evening more or less midway through this period, we were all sitting about waiting for the party to begin, although we were the party. That sudden impulse which would propel us into merriment had not yet arrived. Dima was footling with the piano. We thought he might be playing Glinka. We had become fractious, for we could no longer be certain what in the small hours had been said or merely thought. What we'd done to one another or merely dreamt of doing.

René had just arrived, coat burnished with frost. He began to take it off, before realising that the gesture would be worse than pointless. The space heater was older than we were and moving it from Dima's room would probably break it. Carly got up to embrace him, ruffling his ginger hair like a beloved pet, then leading him over to sit at her feet as she reassumed her place next to Alexa.

René said, 'I had a revelation last night and now it's gone again. I can feel all around its outline like it's a missing tooth, but I can't remember it.' He sat holding his notebook and running his thumb along the pages in the way you'd flick a pack of cards.

Luke was going through the carrier bags René had set down and distributing the wine inside. He was in one of his gaunt phases and had likely been going for days. We were seldom sure how much of his demeanour was mere raffishness and how much genuine dissipation.

He said, 'You just need more inspiration, then it won't matter what you've lost.'

'I want a glass of that, I brought it,' René snapped. Luke had a tendency to treat René's things like they were his own, which extended to stealing René's clothes and sleeping in his bed. They saw each other every day and spent most of them arguing.

'Do you remember the thought process before you got to the idea? That usually helps me.' Alexa, without Pavel for once, was curled up on the only good chair.

We suspected Dima of keeping it for her because they shared a mother tongue. The rest of us were splayed on old mattresses and all-weather beanbags liberated from a nearby beer garden.

'I was high as balls, so no.'

'The solution to that problem is more drugs,' said Carly, reapplying her lipstick in the only reflective surface to be found – the kitchen knife we used to rack up lines. René gave a sceptical cough.

'What? I'm convinced there are thoughts and memories I can only access when I'm in a similar state to the one where I made them.'

Luke said, 'That's creepy, having thoughts and not knowing you've had them. I'm pretty sure I just don't think past a certain point.'

'Perhaps you don't, but you're a special case.' Carly pursed her lips and put down the knife.

Luke took a swig of wine from the bottle. 'So you were fully compos mentis when I came across you fingerblasting Alexa in the stairwell last week?'

'Enjoyed the show, did you?' she asked tartly.

'I was trying to get past you to the door, I had to pick up from João.'

'How strange, we didn't hear you there. You had three other doors to choose from.'

Alexa ignored them both and said, 'Your revelation's still in there somewhere, René, but you couldn't be aware of all your thoughts all the time, you'd go mad.' Alexa's parents had come through London, bearing many much-missed treats. She tore the cellophane off the black and gold cigarettes which had become our favourites. 'Think of this house, no single person could inhabit every room at once.'

Dima put his elegant musician's hands together in a gesture of prayer. She threw a cigarette at him and it bounced off his steepled fingers, rolling away. Luke snatched that one up and lit it before Dima could, so she threw him another. He closed the keyboard lid and proceeded to ash into a jam jar that had been resting on top of the piano.

René asked, 'Isn't that what artists do? Parcel themselves out into lots of perspectives at once?'

Alexa turned to Dima. 'What was the old story about Koshchei?'

'I think he hid his heart in seven pieces, I don't remember exactly.'

'Wasn't that Voldemort?' Carly raised an eyebrow.

René laughed. 'Where do you think she got the idea of a divided soul? Everything's been done, every story's been told. My grandfather used to say that once, as a young man living in Brittany, he saw his friend waiting for him outside in the cold. He knew the man was on a boat to Tangier at the time, but there he was, up to his knees in snow, staring through the window at him.'

Carly asked, 'Was his friend dead?'

'No, but they had unfinished business, he claimed the friend felt their parting so deeply it split him in two for a moment. Then again, my grandfather loved tall tales.'

In the corner of the room, Luke yawned, then stretched and said, 'Not everything's been done . . .'

'Stop trying to make me do opium with you, Luke. It's just shit heroin.' René took the opportunity to seize back his wine and poured a great slug of it into a chipped tumbler. Luke's pupils were very large, especially in the low light.

Alexa, who'd decided she got to needle Dima as her price for the cigarettes, said, 'He'll do it with you. You wish it was the nineteenth century, don't you, Dimochka?'

'Such a great time to be a Tatar, my family loved it.'

Luke ignored them and carried on. 'I just think every-one should try everything once . . . since Carly's having such trouble painting men, maybe she should sleep with one.'

René choked on his wine a bit, then tore a page out of the notebook to blot his mouth.

Carly stretched out her hand against the candles and examined the way they transformed her skin into rosy windows between the metacarpals.

'Why should I put myself through something I know I won't enjoy?'

'But you can't know, that's the point.'

'I have an imagination.'

Dima chimed in. 'My penis is beyond your imagination.'

This time Alexa threw the lighter at his head and said to Luke, almost without judgement, 'How like a man to believe that not only can every experience be yours, but that you would emerge unchanged and unhurt by any of them.'

Carly slipped the wrap back into her shirt. 'I can either go find the rest of the party or I can find out how it feels to murder somebody.' She picked up her satchel and left the room. As Carly's tread grew quieter down the hallway, we looked round at each other and waited for someone else to speak first.

René turned to Luke. 'What was that?'

'It was just a joke, I was being Devil's advocate.'

'You were being a massive git. You should go and find her and sort it out.'

'Isn't that Alexa's job?'

Alexa said, 'I'd rather not right now, you've really put your foot in it.'

'Guys, this is getting boring. Someone go find her and calm her down, she has the coke.' Dima hadn't moved from the piano, but had made it look so like any of the other pieces of furniture he habitually sprawled over that we'd forgotten he was still sitting at it.

All of us looked pointedly at Luke. He was waxy with exhaustion, but went anyway. This having been re-solved, we moved on to pleasanter pastimes. After finding a dead bird in the grate towards the end of summer, we'd realised the chimneys were not blocked after all. Alexa was busily tearing up back issues of the *LRB* to start a fire. Dima found old furniture online that was free if he would take it away. He chopped it apart in the little courtyard out back, then dragged it up to languish in the corner of the ballroom. For someone who spent most of his life doing very little, he was surprisingly strong. René ran saliva-dampened fingers over the residue left on the knife, as Dima and Alexa began bickering in Russian. The rest of us scrabbled towards the warmth, shucking off our dirty coats. The flames were lively, burning orange, then green when they caught onto pamphlets and brochures hidden among the pages, bifurcating and reuniting and consuming everything that came into contact with them. We began chucking in ticket stubs and balled-up receipts, the detritus of the dying year. None of us would have noticed if René slipped out.

Luke huffed his way along the corridor and tried to find the switch. It had a mouldy brocade trim around it that was peeling off. Nothing happened. He decided to chance it and hoped there would be nothing unexpected on his downward path. The left-hand staircase seemed slightly less

Carly was feeling better now. She had plunged right into the dark of the house like it was deep water shocking herself with the cold in search of another room where there would be idiot friends to commiserate with her about her other idiot friends. The music seemed to get more distant as she moved towards it. She uninviting. A ray of moonlight drooped down into the stairwell from the jagged hole above.

He was so tired it occurred to him he could just pass out and tumble down all however-many flights. That might be more restful. He wanted to vomit. Buffeted by uppers and smoothed by downers, it remained to be seen which of these forces would win out. When was the last time he'd slept? Carly needed to get a grip, it could hardly be the first time someone had suggested to her she might try an experience common to half the human race. More even.

turned and tried to retrace her steps, went down one flight and up another, then came upon a little room she must have missed.

Light was edging out from underneath the door. This must be one of the rooms in which some lights still worked. She pushed it open and saw a divan, with a spineless collected works of Swinburne lying face down on the floor beside it. The walls were covered with cloth hangings. It was hard to see in the low light, but they looked to be patterned with vines, flowers, fruit and birds and seemed to be keeping out the worst of the cold. There was even a blanket crumpled up behind the divan. She started tapping out meditative lines from the wrap onto the back of the book.

He and René often joked the only reason they didn't sleep together was they couldn't agree who'd be bottom. If they did ever go there, it would clearly mean more to whichever of them had to take it. Yet Luke persisted in flirting with him; the attention still felt good.

Having reached the ground floor, he heard a creak that suggested someone far above was coming down this way too. Luke was sure Carly couldn't have gone too far ahead of him, maybe that was her coming down the stairs right now, though the tread was a bit too heavy for it to be her. He hoped she would calm down and let him

The blanket smelled of damp but at least it wasn't cobwebby. Hopefully Alexa would find her soon, and they could have the argument Luke had been trying to provoke. She got on well with Pavel, but it was becoming difficult that she didn't want him too. She needed to be more than a diversion he could send away.

For a moment, Carly didn't notice René standing in the doorway. She looked up at him and started laughing. 'Where did you find those? Don't tell me Dima has a whole room of prosthetics.' Baffled, René looked down, as if checking his legs were still there. He mashed his palms against his chest in confusion. Panicking now, he pulled

40

explain how pear-shaped everything had gone.

He and René had run through the bulk order quicker than intended and helped themselves to more than their share. The coke had already been cut with a lot of crap, they couldn't dilute it any further, the Russians knew their powders. Luke tried and failed not to remember his three maxed out credit cards. João was getting unfriendly as it became clear they couldn't give him the second half of the money. They should never have kept the stash so close to hand. João wouldn't stop calling, no matter how hard Luke ignored him.

He rested at the foot of staircase, with his back to

up his T-shirt to find out what had happened.

'Alright, alright luv, get them out fer the lads,' Carly had put the coke down now and was making her way over. 'They're so realistic. How have you got them to stay on like that?' Without thinking, René tried to back away from Carly's finger, but it was too late. She prodded him in the nipple and it visibly hardened. 'What on earth . . .' René turned round and with the door still open, undid his fly with his back to Carly, checked, gasped and turned again, shyly re-buttoning his jeans. He seemed to be appalled at this confirmation that the change was indeed complete.

Carly caught his chin in her hand and turned his

the wall. The shooting pains had returned. He'd been advised to straighten his back out when he felt them, but this made it worse. Hunching over was more comfortable. There was a bronchial feeling as well as a spine feeling, like his lungs were clinging to the back of his ribcage.

Luke could just about make out the shape of someone a little shorter than him descending in the grey darkness.

'Who is it?' No reply, but the shape kept getting nearer. 'Carly? Is that you? I'm sorry, let's sit down and talk about it. Alexa does care about you, you know.' He could hear breathing

face in the light. 'I don't know how you've done it, but you make a very handsome woman.' 'I . . . I started feeling weird on the way here, but I thought I was just feverish. All those endless flights of stairs, I started getting dizzy . . .'

René was making spluttering noises and grasping at his newly generous chest.

Carly had a squeeze. They were definitely breasts.

'Just go with it and enjoy yourself. You might prefer being a woman.' René sat on the edge of the divan, shoulders hunched, as if trying to hide himself. 'Cheer up. Nobody's going to oppress you in here. Have a line.' René did as instructed. He put a finger over his left nostril and sniffed hard to make sure it now, it was definitely a man. 'Dima?' Still nothing but the slow heavy tread down towards him.

Suddenly he remembered João had delivered here. Could he have come in through the back? Could it be one of the small men who sat in the back of João's big white Jeep as it careened round London, grunting and playing on their phones? He legged it.

Round the corner, round another corner, down two flights, into one of the old drawing rooms and through. Fuck, should he lead this guy away from his friends or was there strength in numbers? Keep wheezing, keep going. He really wasn't fit enough for this. Can't go

had all gone in. After a minute's silence, he sat up and raked his fingers through his chin-length ginger curls then tucked a strand back behind his ear.

'At least I'm among friends. Imagine if this had happened somewhere else, like a locker room.' 'Or a job interview.' 'Or an airport.' 'Do you want to go find people and tell them?' 'Not really, I mean, who knows how long this will last.'

Carly smiled slightly, felt a hard look enter her eyes. She pulled him to her by the collar of his T-shirt. 'Are-are-you-sure?' 'Are you sure you can't get coke dick in your current condition?' By way of answer, René removed his jeans, prepared to climb over on out into the street, they'll be empty at this time of year and more men might be waiting in a car. Fuckfuckfuck.

He burst into a bathroom, thinking to barricade himself inside and call Dima. Light and shrieking and shiny flesh. Apparently Sita and Nadia were having a bath together, both drinking champagne out of separate bottles. More shrieking, lots of bubbles. No time to look. He made for the next door into one of the back bedrooms. That should distract his pursuer for a bit.

Luke kept on going anyway, racing upwards now, three steps at a time. Could he lock him in a

top of Carly. She already had her shirt half-off. She caught him by the shoulders and whirled him round so he was supine.

'Let me show you how it is.' She put her mouth on his neck, moving up behind the ear, alternating between hard and soft, felt his legs spasm involuntarily as she slid her hand over the ribcage beneath the underside of his breast. Before he could reach up to pull off the rest of her shirt, she slid out of it, pressed herself against him to keep him warm and took a slender wrist in either hand.

She was kissing the new hollows in his hips now, tracing her tongue along them and laughing to herself at how he writhed.

cupboard somehow, or force him to a standoff? Would anyone miss this guy if he fell off the roof? He could still hear footsteps behind him, and outraged screams from both the girls.

Luke ducked behind a door and felt the figure thundering past him. They had circled back into a less dark part of the house and silhouetted against the moonlight Luke could see from the full cheekbone and sharp jaw that the man was handsome, whoever he was. Luke eased out his phone to call Dima – the battery was on 3%. The man must have seen the glow and came back running the other way.

Yes don'tstopdon'tstop-don'tstop – She didn't stop. He was staring at the hanging on the ceiling. Tulips intertwined with little crescent moons. She left him a grace period, waiting until he looked like he'd regained the ability to think.

'I told you it wasn't all bad.'
'Is it always like that?'
'When the other girl knows what she's doing.'
He gathered her in and kissed her hard and slowly. She could taste what she supposed must be him, familiar-unfamiliar. Carly wrapped her legs around him, stroked his back like he was a horse that had won its race. She wondered with a rush of evil pleasure whether she had dented René's pride in his own prowess.

Luke panicked, pulled the door to, then felt the man ram it with his shoulder. The wood was rotten and Luke doubted it would hold. He rammed it again and Luke heard a crack. If the crack got big enough, he might try to punch right through the door. The man rammed it another time and as he drew back to go again, Luke yanked the door open and slammed it into the man's face as he fell past where the door should have been, catching a glimpse of red hair. It definitely connected, but Luke kept on running. No time to tell if he was concussed or merely stunned when the fucker was so determined to catch up with him. No time to stop and find out if that was who he thought it was. It couldn't be René?

'How would you feel if I took you out for dinner?' Carly wrinkled a nostril, winced, remembering it was raw from coke.
'You really have turned into a woman. I make you come once and you're picking wedding china.'
'Carly, you know and I know this has been a long time overdue.'
'No. It hasn't. I could hardly have predicted you would show up looking so different.'
'You wanted me as well. You said I'm the person you have all your imaginary conversations with.' He reached across the divan for the coke and licked his finger, breasts swinging out as he moved. He was really very pretty, mouth newly bowed and tendrils of dampened red hair escaping from behind his ears.

46

He could taste blood, wrung out of his overtired lungs with the effort of running. Maybe he should lie down and let it happen, whatever it turned out to be. It would never get better, there would always be someone trying to get in too close, wanting too much from him. It wasn't even that he particularly liked drugs anymore, but nothing else was as effective. They annihilated time: no memory of the past, no fear for the future. They shut out the world beyond the house and its determination to impose significance on how he felt.

It would be so much easier just to let it happen. But he suspected it was really going to hurt, in a way that would change

'Are you sure nothing prompted this transformation? It isn't something you've wanted for a while? Because you could have come to me before now, if it was.' René paused, fiddled with the loose strap of his watch. She could see he was considering lying, then remembering how well they knew each other. He said in a small, defeated voice 'no.'
'So this doesn't feel more natural for you?' She ran her index from his collarbone to mid-thigh.
'It feels great.'
'You're avoiding the question.'

'Yes, I would like my body back. My original body. I can't believe you're so hung up on this, it shouldn't matter.'
'My god, you're just like

47

him. Luke kept running, forcing open doors now as he went, hoping to find something to repel him with. An old chair leg would do.

One room was full of wigs and chicken fillets from that time Dima befriended a Spice Girls tribute drag act. Another just had lots of broken hoovers, tubes knotted and tangled in a pile. A third had several scale models of buildings, covered by glass domes.

He wondered if this house was one of them, with a tiny Luke pursued through it, looking at an even tinier model of the house containing an even tinier Luke and René pursuing. The next room he opened, a cloud of

Luke. Your wanting or not wanting it is the only thing that matters.'
'But I want you, and I know you can want men, you have before.'

René was lying on his side, but back in the hunched position. The balls of his feet were cold circles against the tops of her knees. Carly curled around him, pressing her breasts into his shoulder blades and insinuating her arm under his neck. She couldn't believe she had to keep explaining this.

'I'm sorry, OK? I wish I could love you, but I can't. I can't pick up your socks and be introduced as René's girlfriend and commiserate with straight women about how awful their boyfriends are. I can't be acceptable again.'

grey-brown moths rose up and went everywhere, he had to race through with his eyes and mouth shut to stop them getting in. Luke could still feel their old-cloth filth against his skin as he hurtled, panting, into another corridor.

He could hear René gaining on him, tread shaking the floorboards under Luke's feet as he got closer, but there was a light spilling out from one of the rooms, it was the third door on the left. Finally, here might be a place where he could rest, to meet the fate he both desired and feared.

'You won't be "picking up my socks", I'm probably tidier than you are.'
'It's not about socks, or vaginas, it's about existing at a slant.' Carly could hear shouting a long way off inside the house. She wondered if someone had broken another window.

She considered her position. 'If you're still stuck like that in a few months' time, I'll take you out for dinner, you'll know what I mean by then.'
He rolled over, nestled in closer to Carly, tucking his head under her chin and breathed in deeply. She stroked his hair and thought of all the joy and disappointment that lay in wait for him.

The door burst open and Luke half ran, half fell in through it. Carly sprang out of bed, not caring she was naked, about to give Luke the telling-off of a lifetime. She couldn't allow him to think she'd proved his point. For a moment, Carly was sure she could see René right behind him. She turned back confused to René on the divan, but no one was there.

Luke stopped wheezing and composed himself, shuttering the terror that had been plain a moment before. He asked, 'Who've you got in here, then? She had great tits. Is she hiding behind the bed?'

Carly looked around, and seeing no one, lifted up the hangings, found only peeling walls behind them. She rounded on Luke, 'What were you running from? Did you manage to piss Alexa off as well?'

Carly and Luke came back to us hand in hand. We were pleased they'd made up. We couldn't understand why they were so horrified to find René sitting quietly in the ballroom, scribbling in his notebook.

A Wolf in the Temple

A man once prophesied I had the eyes of a thief. He never said how much would be taken from me.

I was still a girl when I was sold, and so my childhood was stolen by my first husband, who hurt and then insulted me. My foster father killed him for his insults, but took my home from me by doing so, for after that my father's house was home no longer. My second husband was the choice of necessity, that I might make a home of my own, but this failed also. His rivalry with my foster father took all the pleasant memories of my youth and sullied them. It became as clear as the waters of the Grjótá that my foster father felt what no man should feel for a girl he has raised as his own. Each of them I used to kill the other, like two hands washing themselves clean. My third and last husband was Gunnar, whom I chose for myself. Another man stole him, but nobody would believe an outcast like me, if I told them how.

When I saw Gunnar at the Althing he had recently returned from abroad, where he'd been richly rewarded by the Norwegian king for fighting off raiders at sea. He brought back with him a magic axe which never missed and made a ringing noise presaging it would soon take a man's life. His hair was long and as fair as the snow that even in summer lies on top of the black mountains. His cheeks were as pink as the belly of a freshly cut salmon. I knew his name and reputation before I placed myself in his way, asking to be told stories of his travels. I'd dressed in my finest clothes, but he did not show much interest in me. I feared I was already too old to stake my claim on a man like him, that my own killings had tired me out. It was only when I warned him I was hard to please in the matter of husbands that he began talking interestedly.

Here, I thought, is a man who likes a challenge. He would not be deterred by the unfair account of me he would doubtless receive from my father.

Gunnar's best friend, Njal, came to my wedding party and his wife Bergthora helped to serve at the feast. If I'd known then what I know now, I would have poisoned every cup and drinking horn and died gladly with the rest of them. Njal was older than Gunnar, but still beardless and soft-handed. He did not like to fight, but Njal was so cunning he could influence the decisions of the law courts years in advance. He upheld land claims and brokered oaths and gave judgements on how much blood money was to be paid out for various men. He also read omens and foretold the future, which should be a task for women only. It was said Njal knew how he himself would die one day. He and Gunnar were sworn brothers, but no brothers I've ever seen behave like that when they believe themselves unobserved.

He and Bergthora came often to our farmstead and we, in turn, to theirs. I spent long hours standing over the servant girls to make sure Njal and his wife would have nothing but the crispest morsels of lamb and softest skyr when they visited us. We laughed and sang and talked late into the night. Bergthora was taller than Njal and broader in the shoulders, often preferring loose britches to the layers of skirts I always wore. She had shining red hair and a dimple in her chin. She liked challenging me to drink toasts to our husbands, to our glorious ancestors, and to the spirits of the land. I would usually stumble up to the loft barely able to see, but Njal and Gunnar were so brazen I couldn't have missed what passed between them. I still remember one winter night at Hlíðarendi, coming round from my stupor in one of our high seats to look across and see Bergthora cleaning her nails with an ivory pick, while Gunnar sat in Njal's lap and kissed him. Njal's hands were in his hair, while Gunnar clasped him about the waist. I didn't understand how she could put up with it, she'd borne him three sons and was a woman of good family. If it had been Bergthora he'd betrayed me with, I could at least have fought her, although I would have lost.

When it was just us two alone, Gunnar would hardly touch me. He asked my advice on the running of the farm or exercising his claims to cut timber on shared land, but he slept beside me for warmth only. I tried everything, buying pastes from pedlar women to whiten my skin, reciting bawdy verses about troll-wives, touching him in the early morning when he was half asleep. The only thing that worked was begging him for children, and I suspected he only tried to succeed at that so he'd have an excuse to leave me alone again. I started refusing to go on his visits with him, saying that Njal did not give Bergthora the respect he owed a wife and Gunnar could ride out alone for all I cared.

I was mending the trim on an old cloak in one of our back rooms when I heard two pairs of footsteps coming to my door. I had sent the servants to the other end of the house, not wishing to hear their idle jokes or descriptions of their young men elsewhere in the valley. One showed Bergthora in and lingered outside till I closed the door in her face. We waited until she realised we were listening for her to leave. I rose to go through the motions of greeting Bergthora, but she pressed both hands down on my shoulders. Her lips were soft and soursweet with brennivín. I wanted to. Winter is long and a well-fed servant knows better than to whisper about her mistress outside the house. I wanted to. But the men had sent Bergthora and if I accepted, I could no longer claim Gunnar for myself. I wanted to, but I pushed her away.

The next time we were invited to their farm, he told me that if I intended to keep trying for a child, I would go along and behave myself. Bergthora wouldn't look me in the eye, and I found I'd been demoted from the seat of honour by her side, in favour of her kinswoman. Gunnar ignored the insult, and I felt rage build up in my belly like hunger, a burning hunger great enough to consume everything I saw. I was determined to shame her as she had humiliated me. When she brought round the water, I seized her hand by the wrist and said loudly,

'You and Njal are so alike. You have the hands of a man, with broken nails on every finger and Njal is as beardless as you.' Then I let it drop back into the bowl, splashing water on her shirt.

She replied, 'That may be so, but I have never caused my husband's death.'

All the way home, I kept on at Gunnar, goading him that despite his reputation as the bravest man in Iceland, I knew him to be no man at all. What was the point of him? My treatment as his wife was a reflection of his status, but clearly he didn't care about abasing himself.

Since I could not prevail with him, I started a feud between my bondsmen and Bergthora's. Small men are the easiest to rouse to murder, when their manliness is challenged, for often they have nothing else beyond that. Any man who cares for his honour is easily moved. It pleased me to imagine Bergthora wringing those broad hands of hers when she heard about the latest of her servants to die at the sword of one of mine. I would not be ignored. The feud progressed until our dependent minor kinsmen could be sent out to the slaughter, but still Njal and Gunnar were determined to make peace. I longed to set them at each other's throats. He had promised me the love of his body and his heart also, but he cared more for his dog than he did for me.

The old stories say that the wolf Fenrir was young and weak when the gods tortured his father and drove away his mother, though soon he grew large enough to threaten their belief in their own strength. Asgard was the only home he'd ever known, but they said he was destined to be a monster, for they had good reason to fear him. When the gods bound Fenrir in a rope made from seven impossible things, they told him it was a game. Though he was young, he had already learnt he wasn't welcome and refused to be bound unless Tyr placed his hand in Fenrir's mouth. So afraid were the gods, that Tyr sacrificed his hand to keep the wolf out of Asgard. But Fenrir will have his revenge, for at the end of time, he will burst his fetters and devour them all.

The next fight I picked for Gunnar was with Otkel, a man who had powerful friends and many relatives. Some of these relatives had already been bested in the courts by Gunnar, so there was little chance he and Njal could come to terms with them. I sent a servant to raid this man's storehouse and burn it down. People in our valley thought I stole out of boredom or greed, or simply because I had always been a thief, as the prophecy said. Gunnar paid me some mind then, even though he showed it by slapping me for stealing. The second feud had already begun and he couldn't stop this one. I loved him best when he rode out with his jaw set hard under his helmet and his axe ringing. He would sate it with the bodies of our neighbours and I waited up to wash the blood out of his clothes myself. How like a real man he was, when I made him one.

After more than twenty men had been killed, the chieftains tried to exile Gunnar. Even Njal told him to go, saying they would both live to be old men if he could only wait out a few years abroad. But Gunnar couldn't bear to leave the farm where he had been so happy. It's said that the last time they parted, Gunnar asked Njal to raise our sons, as if I could not do it.

The night his enemies attacked the house, we were sleeping up in the loft with his mother. Not long after our second son was born, his mother had started to complain she needed Gunnar's help at night. I was seldom alone with him again. I was still asleep when they climbed up on the thatch and tried to get in through the windows. I woke to cries, squelches and thuds as Gunnar stuck his sword up into the roof again and again. He impaled them as they clung there, then pulled it back through to let them roll off and hit the ground. Next, he started shooting arrows at the men who were waiting outside. Realising they'd never defeat him while he could shoot, one man jumped down through the roof and gave his life to sever Gunnar's bowstring. He asked his mother and me to cut off and braid together two strands of my hair to make a replacement. But why should I have ruined my remaining beauty? His hair was as long as mine when unbound, but clearly it was more important that Njal should run his hands through it and think all of it equally fine. Gunnar said he wouldn't ask me twice.

It was a windless night, when I rode back to Hlíðarendi. This was my last chance to see Gunnar in his mound, for his axe had started ringing, which meant he was soon to be avenged. I heard the silence only dead things make. My mare tried to turn back, but I kicked her till she ran in a circle round the grave. Faster and faster, till my vision blurred and the cold air caused my eyes to stream. The grave cracked open and I saw Gunnar sitting in his mound. His beautiful skin was grey and his lips were blue. The mound was full of flames, twining and writhing as if he rested in a bed of snakes, but they didn't burn his flesh.

I turned and saw that Njal was at my side. We looked for a long time at the man both of us had loved and I had killed. Gunnar looked back with eyes unseeing. Njal shed no tears and didn't seem angry. He reached across the gap between our horses to touch my arm and said, 'When I go to join him in the fire, who will you have left to hate?'

Lick the Dust

When you misplace something in the library here, it stays lost for a very long time. The eighteenth-century catalogue that alerted me to the book's existence was brought up from the vaults by mistake. It had a similar order number to another, more exhaustive version written by the same antiquarian twenty years later, after he had acquired more of Simon Cypriano's library for the university at auction. Since the catalogue was in front of me, I thought I might have a look at this early attempt to document the university's ever-expanding collection of occult medieval manuscripts. I expected to find only a shorter list of the same books, but perhaps the antiquarian had been more clear-sighted in his youth and included better descriptions. Two thin pages were stuck together, although the numeration skipped over them, concealing this at first. I looked around at all the diligent indifferent heads lowered over mahogany lecterns, like buoys bobbing in the sea. Very slowly, so as not to attract the attention of those oafs they call librarians, I pried the leaves apart with a fingernail. At first I feared that I was simply destroying an irregularly made page for nothing, and then, as I saw there was more writing, thrilled that my suspicion had been correct. The hand was cramped and spidery, but from what I could make out, the two hidden pages described an unknown book by the Great Magus Cypriano, which the antiquarian had tucked away in Lord Kenelm's library on the other side of Oxford. He provided details of the binding, but also warned that this book should be handled very carefully, perhaps not at all. What a superstitious idiot, to be living in the Enlightenment but still behaving like the men he studied! I hoped this might be the lost book that Cypriano was rumoured to have written before his disappearance. If I were to find it, it would be the making of my career – or at least, salvation from early and permanent obscurity.

But now the catalogue pages were unstuck, for anyone to see. What if Professor Kelly learnt about the book and kept all the credit? Or that sly bitch Agnes? She took everything that was mine. Agnes was picked to convene the conferences and invited to symposia. Agnes won the M. R. James scholarship and I had to get by on a couple of crappy little funds and countless hours spent teaching *Guthlac* to undergraduates barely literate in modern English. None of her papers were particularly brilliant, but she was prepared to flirt with the great and good. That was how she got in with everyone, a light touch on the arm and some confidences that would cost her nothing. That was how she had tried to get in with me, back when she thought I could be of any use to her.

I grabbed a larger bound manuscript from my pile and made a show of heaving it onto the lectern, sliding the little catalogue into my thick woollen cardigan as I did so. No one would miss it. I stayed another half-hour, noting down unusual manicules and measuring the gutters. I'd spent so much of my life on tasks like these, I was becoming sure I could tell hair side from flesh side on the vellum. It was the only skin contact I had these days, after all.

After I'd placed the other manuscripts on the reshelving trolley, I went to rub out the catalogue's call number in the orders book, since the more popular version they should have brought me remained in the vaults and I was hardly about to alert them to their error. The petty scum who run this place still insist we come in to write out our requests by hand, no matter how inconvenient this might be for us. Fortunately, they have also forbidden us the use of pens. A mechanical pencil is enough to make them send you back down to the lockers. Completely erasing the request would leave a tell-tale gap, so I decided I would write in Agnes's name instead and the call number for a richly illuminated book of love lyrics. Kelly would be bound to see it and assume she was wasting precious time showing off the university's treasures to dilettantes. Both of our DPhils had overrun, mine because the work demanded strictest accuracy, hers because she was always jetting off around the world. All the enthusiasm I had once felt for my thesis had long ago withered away, but what remained was a cold determination to finish before she did.

It was already three, Lord Kenelm's library would be closed before I could get there, so early the next morning I began my search. It took weeks. I should have been focussing on my edits, but I knew Cypriano's book was in there. I searched every shelf several times, facing down timewasters when they wouldn't move. The cloistered hush among the dark wooden shelves, smelling of mildew and resin, has a perverse attraction for those people least interested in working. Couples request books to Lord Kenelm so they can have study dates somewhere atmospheric; I don't know why they let undergrads in there at all. I gave myself eye strain and my knees ached from crawling along the lower shelves, but I found it. Tucked away in a little alcove in the upper gallery, it had a golden chimera tooled into the dark blue binding.

I picked up the book and hurried with it into the darkest corner of the library I could find. I could not help but notice it was very light for a book of its size. But there was Cypriano's sigil, embossed on the cover. The leather was soft and worn, but still very supple. I'll admit it, I was trembling. I thought: *this will show Kelly, this will show them all.* I unlatched the metal clasps that held the book shut. Could this be an exhaustive treatise on herbs and spirits? Perhaps the account of his life which some scholars believed they had found references to in other works? Proof he was spying for the king?

In the centre of the book-shaped box lay a black, charred-looking thing. I leant closer, trying to make out what it was, my mind riffling through all the diagrams and illustrations I had ever seen. I started back, feeling like something had grabbed my stomach and twisted it. The wooden lid clacked shut and I had to clamp my lips tight, so as not to spit vomit on the binding. It was a Hand of Glory.

I knew from my reading that these were made from the left hands of hanged criminals, to lend the power of invisibility to living thieves. Blaise Goethius wrote that he once saw Cypriano use a Hand to steal back some love letters he had written to his patron's youngest daughter. But Goethius also thought he could keep water demons in his privy and that drinking tincture of mercury would help him live past a hundred. There was one theory that Cypriano had been so exasperated by Goethius's effusive admiration of his prowess as to repent and enter a monastery on returning to Spain, though most reputable scholars agreed that his disappearance from history was because he had been poisoned in Mantua.

The book-box itself was worthless, except as a curio. He could have bought this and had it bound anywhere in Smithfield. But the Hand would need further examination, before I could be sure what best to do. It occurred to me that I might sell it secretly, the price I could fetch for such a gruesome and rare thing even without the illustrious history of its owner would keep me afloat for several years if I couldn't get a funded postdoc. I took a handkerchief out of my pocket, making sure not to come into contact. Who knew how fragile it might be? The Hand was stuck to a slip of parchment with Cypriano's writing on it. Now this might really be of interest, and could plausibly have fallen out from somewhere else. Attached as it was, I picked it up along with the Hand, placing them gently in the deep breast pocket inside my jacket. As I buttoned the jacket closed, I could have sworn I felt it nestling up to me.

Huddled in the privacy of my room after informal hall, I took it out. It was intact, a small hand but a sturdy one, so old the muscles had dried up into wood-like ridges and whorls. The high arch of the palm, the delicacy of the fingertips – for a moment I allowed myself to wonder if this had been a woman's hand, but that was hardly likely. So few women ever got caught. Using steel tweezers and my magnifying glass, I unfurled the parchment slip to read it.

If thou wishest to use this Hande that hath served me so well and so readilie go thou to thy Holy Bookes. Thou may find there Isaiah 49 and Psalme 72 that is King Solomon's Psalme. Burn thou these and blow the foule airs upon this Hande between the hours of compline and matins that it may know thy maistrie.

I had not come across anything like this in the works of his contemporaries. Checking my watch, I saw I was within the appointed hours of night for a little experiment. More out of silliness than anything else, I took down the King James Bible, sitting unused on my shelf since Kelly had publicly humiliated me for using it in footnotes instead of Douay-Rheims.

Leafing through in such a hurry that the scritta paper tore, I found the necessary verses. I took a lighter from the wobbly bedside drawer I'd been provided with by the college and followed Cypriano's instructions, fearing that

I might set the Hand alight and so spoil all my chances. Rooms in St Bernadine's were so high-ceilinged that I would have some time before the smoke detector began to bleep.

Nothing happened. I tried again, feeling foolish, then exhaled a deep sigh, hoping to blow the burning pages out. In the warmth, the Hand stretched and flexed its pointed fingers, shrugging off some of its ancient crust. I felt the nub of wrist turning through the handkerchief. In a practised-looking gesture it drew the flames to itself, coiling them in like ribbons until there was a blue-white ball of fire resting in its palm.

I felt light-headed, but calm enough. The only question was what to do now? I already had the most valuable thing I could think of in my possession, but I decided that I should still test it out. I held it uplifted like a torch, and reaching for the doorknob to my set with my free hand, I found that it passed right through and out into the corridor. It didn't hurt, though I could feel the grainy solidity of the door as I pushed through it. Exhilarated, I hurried down to the darkened quad, lamplight orange on the cobbles, and saw I cast no shadow. The porter was making his dumpy way back to the lodge, muttering about a party on another staircase. Apparently, some great wit had decided to cover all the portraits in stick-on googly eyes. I followed him, close behind. There was a stone near my feet, glossy black and the perfect size for throwing. Struck, he wheeled round with a face that would terrify the most entitled day-tripper, but looked right through me. It had worked! Then, I noticed that the flame was beginning to shrink and flicker, the Hand curling to close over it. There was no time to draw breath and light it again. I started running. I had to get back into the stairwell before the light went out.

I practised with the Hand every night; now it knew who its mistress was, all I needed to do was take it from the drawer and breathe upon the shrunken palm. I walked through all the sets in my corridor and watched their occupants weeping, working, making love. The lengths of time the Hand allowed me to remain unseen were variable, so I stayed cautious. Even in pitch-black rooms, that roiling ball of flame allowed me to observe everything. There was nothing so pure as being in things but not of them. It was what I had once loved about the past, the intimacy of studying other human beings and uncovering what had long remained secret, without any messy interaction. My first thought had been to creep outside and back into the libraries to access the special collections in their vaults. However, I found I could not bypass the wall around St Bernadine's. It was even older than the college and had been built and re-built in successive layers. Some people said a woman had been walled up alive in there, to ensure it never fell.

It was around this time that Kelly called us in to announce another batch of funding had been released for fourth years. Agnes was wearing an azure blue coat I'd never seen her in before, with strands of golden hair pulled back into a loose bun, like she fancied herself the

Madonna in a rose window. When she asked me how my work was going, I answered, 'Well enough.'

'I'm glad to hear that. I'm sure both of us will do our best. I enjoyed your article on the marginalia in Rais 157, you know.'

'I think I saw a mention of Nottingham in an old issue of *Manuskripte*, if you're still interested in citing him.'

I knew perfectly well she couldn't read German. I'd hated Agnes since the day I met her. She always looked as if she was lit up from inside, but now I had my candle in the dark.

The funding forms were long and tedious, they asked us lots of sentimental questions about our reasons for studying and how it would 'benefit the community'. I wanted to know what Agnes had put on hers. By now I was pretty sure I could make it into the next quad, up several flights of stairs and back, with lots of time to spare. If I knew what she had written, I could improve on it, make her words sound trite and dull compared to mine. I needed that money badly, while she was splashing out on new clothes. Her room was neat, with posters of the Mappa Mundi and sections from the Book of Kells. I passed the flame over her sleeping face. I'd thought she would look different asleep, that her expression would reveal her for the calculating slut I knew her to be. She remained soft-cheeked, slightly smiling but otherwise unreadable. Her nightwear was unexpectedly demure.

I opened up her laptop, humming on the desk. Just as I had found the parts I wanted, she sat right upright and asked:

'Who's there?'

As if I could have answered. Then it came to me that I might have some fun with Agnes in other ways than surpassing her. I picked up her shoes and threw them. Flicked the table lamp on and off until it broke. Lifted up the furniture so it looked like it was floating. Her screams were echoing in the corridor as I ran.

Soon the bags under her eyes were stained almost as deep as mine. Her lovely hair began to thin and Kelly mentioned her with exasperation in our meetings, the way he must usually have been talking about me. I didn't visit every night – sometimes she slunk off to her boyfriend's house in Jericho. Besides, I had begun to find that I was often short of breath. My extended sessions with the Hand left me gasping to the point of fainting for many hours after. Often, I thought I could feel the sharp points of its fingernails pushing inside me, like five roundels branded onto my heart.

At night when I was minding my own business reading, I heard it tapping in the drawer, asking to come out. I didn't like to overindulge the Hand, I was the one in charge here, but the thought of its company was not unpleasant. Sometimes I came just to watch her. She usually lay on her left side, curled around a pillow, or flat on her back, exhaling little whistling snores. That rosebud mouth empty of platitudes for once. A corkboard of trophies hung from the back of her door – smiley photos with her vapid-looking friends, congratulatory cards, love notes from her admirers. The more you are given, the more entitled you feel to take. I wondered how often over the course of our lives she would snatch everything I'd worked for away from me.

One night, I found that she was not alone; she'd asked her boyfriend to stay with her. But I was not afraid of the captain of the rowing team. In fact, she had provided me with a wonderful opportunity. I climbed up onto the bed and knelt over her chest, one knee to pin each arm. With my free hand I covered her mouth before she could even think to scream. Rory slumbered on beside her, feeling nothing. She must have worn him out. When he woke up with her body in the morning, there would be no one else to blame. She let out a ragged gasp as I slid my hand down to clasp her throat. *Let her find out how it feels to go breathless.* Her body bucked beneath me, the edges of her lips were turning blue. This was the most beautiful she had ever looked and I would be the only one to see it. The Hand was squirming in my hand, like it could enjoy the spectacle, its ball of flame rhythmically flaring and shrinking almost to nothing. How long it was taking her to die. Then the expression on her face changed from terror into rage. I knew the Hand had failed me and I loosened my grip in shock. She shouted my name, her voice hoarse with damage. This, finally, was enough to wake Rory up.

I sprinted through two quads, not much liking my chances. The moon was nearly full and if I couldn't get back in time, there would not be enough darkness to hide in. The dining hall was thick with oak-panelled gloom, I waited there, crouched under the high table, panting.

Were those Rory's footsteps I could hear echoing in the corridor above? From the vantage of the dais, I could see all the way into the kitchens – and out! Some sloppy washer-up had left the door into the street wide open. My ruinous battels had been worth the money after all. I blew frantically trying to relight the flame, and eventually it caught. I could hide myself in the library if I hurried. The pre-dawn streets were crammed with students in clubwear and silly costumes, laughing with each other. More and more of them pressed in behind me, then a huge crowd came surging down Parks Road, carrying me away from the library. I remembered it was May Day. I was jostled by Morris dancers and shoved by boys in suits. Girls with hair down to their waists begged rollies from each other and Green Men on stilts walked high above the throng. It was impossible to get past them. I was being pushed inexorably towards Magdalen. The tower was full of hidden choristers, who made it sound as if it was the stones themselves that sang. The sun was coming up.

I tried to blend in, putting the Hand back in my pocket and slowing to a saunter. Nobody was paying attention, they'd been drinking all night and wouldn't notice me flickering back into view. The music ended and the sermon began, so the crowd began to disperse, as uninterested in the tradition's meaning as it had been compelled by its ambiance. As the crowd thinned, I looked behind me to see Rory shoving through the crowd. He had not yet spotted me, but soon he would. In a panic, I shoved too, hoping to get as far as Cowley and wait in a cafe there for the daylight to convince him Agnes was going mad. I was halfway across the bridge when I saw Kelly coming down St Clements. I owed him a whole chapter of corrections, he would want to stop and talk. Rory was catching up behind me. I wheeled around, trapped. Some drunken idiots were teetering on the outside edge of Magdalen Bridge, readying themselves to jump. I vaulted past them, straight down into the water.

The other jumpers plunged in either side of me, their impact ripping at my clothes. In the dim green light I saw the Hand float up and away from me and tried to catch at it. It opened its fingers wide once more, as if it thought it could make fire down here . . . The fire was in my lungs!

The Hand had me where it wanted, I felt it jerking at my limbs with invisible chains like I was its puppet. I tried to kick off my sodden shoes to keep from sinking further. The more I resisted, the harder it tried to pull my remaining breath from my body. It was so hot inside my ribs I beat the heels of my hands against my breastbone, growing dizzy as it drained the air from my blood. I saw it flexing, writhing with delight. No longer able to hold my breath, I opened my lips and in an instant the Hand darted into my open mouth, scrabbling and clawing as I choked. Bony fingers cut into my tongue as I desperately tried to pull it out. I could feel it dissolving, strips of flesh and cinder floating loose before me as it crawled down my throat.

'Are you alright, miss? I expect you've learnt your lesson. We've a few brave souls that try it every May Day, it always goes the same. You're lucky we're not giving out cautions this year.'

The policeman, having decided that was sufficient, moved along the riverbank to deliver a version of his lecture to other sopping revellers wrapped in golden foil blankets.

This was no time for us to sit around, Agnes was still at the college and we had work to do.

Pretty Rooms

We, who once were united, now are scattered. The places we reside are almost as diverse as the places from which we came. We were chosen for our strength, resilience and price, but mainly for our beauty. We held out for decades, welcoming new members among our ranks, but were seldom reduced. We came in many shapes and sizes, small enough to be held in one hand or bigger than a man; some of us were hewn from once-living wood, while others were pulled from the ground and fixed in fire, or beaten with hammers until their final form was attained. Some among us are clever fakes, and younger than they pretend, while others seem plain, but hold great value. We are by no means exceptional, we are not worthy of national, or even local attention. To those who loved us, we were sufficient.

A few of us came first with the man to his new home, worn from the past half-century of use, but ready to be admired again in our sparse arrangement. He would trail admiring fingers, surprised at the thrill of possession. Home was remade, and, with some transitory items, that was all that was necessary. He cared for us, but only as representatives of his newly sanctioned freedom. We were not often seen by others, though sometimes we felt more weight in the bed and hairpins along the nightstand. We injured no one.

And she kept returning, hanging her coats in the wardrobe and hiding her valise by the trunk. One day we were all wrapped in sheets and loaded together, alongside other things with which we were soon mingled. Some of us found new companions, stacked on top of one another or arranged side-by-side in alcoves. Soon, these combinations seemed the most natural thing in the world. United, it became difficult to recall which of us exactly had arrived from his, or from hers or had been sent as gifts.

She remained with us and moved among us almost ceaselessly. We shone and gleamed and sparkled according to our means. Guests admired us and she was praised for our immaculacy. We were perfected by her so as to make a show of his perfections. She loved us too, all except the desk. She spent many hours there, scratching through sheets of paper to the wood and staining it with ink-blotches. Its lid became a mass of blue-black grooves tunnelling through white smears and gummed detritus. Sometimes she would kick its finely turned legs, though this always seemed to hurt her more.

Her restlessness was turned on us, in the form of meticulous diagrams and new arrivals every few months. More rooms than they could move through, she decorated and improved. We were adjusted endlessly, to sit faded in ever-brighter lights. The building itself was altered to our benefit. We were selected around each other, so that not a single piece was out of place. We became unified by her design, were uniquely hers despite our varied origins. He smiled on us and deemed us most suitable among her occupations. Redistributed, there was more space, although the house was not yet full.

First the creatures came, ripping brocade and clawing tassels. Whole rooms smothered in a fog of satin dander, maybe she preferred that effect. Then some of us were reconfigured in new shades, old boxes dragged back out into consciousness. The children stained every place that they could reach. The smallest of us waited out the invasion on higher shelves, but little hands tracked filth across our surfaces and pulled at loosening threads. She touched us consolingly at night, tried to make him see the dents made in our wood, but soon gave up. Hordes of ugly items passed through and did not return. We were much diminished by this time, the watermarks and scratch marks remain to tell strange histories of violence. Some of us were forever broken.

Eventually things slowed again; for a short while there was a programme of repair. We were polished and sanded, regained a little glamour, a little respectability. Patterns of affection were renewed. Resinated dust was eked carefully out of crannies. She stayed mainly in the garden, watching and resting. He was away a long time. Soon, however, yet more change came upon us. Metal parts and sterile draperies invaded. He was downstairs, surrounded by a different sort of activity. We were imbued with disinfecting odours. We saw many scenes and remained in formation. Within the Chinese prints, all four seasons continued reigning separately.

It was quiet with us, apart from the beetles, boring steadily into everything and leaving trails of fawn-coloured chip. Layers of grime began to settle, mirrors blurred and blackened. Mould snuck up along the backs of curtains and into furtive corners. Tiny silver boxes multiplied, to be moved beyond the grasp of another wave of hands. Silver handles crowded themselves along walls and stairwells to assist her. The bathroom cabinet became filled beyond its capacity, though she no longer minded. She did not seem to see beyond the small fields of cleanliness where she resided most often. We were too many in his absence.

The children returned to walk among us at their full heights, grown to scale with us at last. We felt their fingerprints in the dust. One day we would be theirs, they said. Early attachments were transformed into iron promises. The curlicued faces on a Jacobean chest were not-quite-kissed.

After some time she became like one of us in her stillness.

Again we were packed and shrouded. They separated us, dragged old papers and a white dress from their hidden places, so they could be sent down to anonymous caverns of shared storage. One shelf contains the memory of her poems, never reprinted. Lost treasures were unearthed again, only to be passed over with a laughing shrug. Some of us were given away and others left out worthless in the rain.

We remain dispersed forever, barring some familial cataclysm that might allow for reconsolidation. We make up a network of half-remembered comfort, stretched wide across the country and the seas. In foreign contexts we have lost our functions. Handled relic-like, it would be easy to forget our former existence. But at night the old house remains with all of us, and we assume our former places. Although they cannot hear us, we creak and settle in the dwellings of the past.

Ingratitude

It was not a significant birthday on which my mother called me into her study to discuss my inheritance. Rose and Jenny were playing in the hall, one jumping from the stairs in pursuit and the other waiting by the drawing room door for the cue to run. When they saw me, the twins made a kind of war-cry and took off, darting in opposite directions, so only one of them could be caught at a time. I touched translucent smears on the banister and smelt my fingers. Linseed. They'd been going through my things again. At ten they were too old for this kind of game.

I had shown Rose how to prepare paint just last week, thinning it with white spirit and adding the oil for extra gloss. She'd marvelled at the bright cadmium yellows and deep cobalt as they sank into the small canvas we'd stretched together. Jenny was more interested in making elaborate monsters out of clay, though she wasn't happy enough with any yet to fire them.

'Stop dawdling out there, I haven't got all day!'

My mother busied herself opening and shutting drawers, pulling them out so far they threatened to fall, then shoving them back in with a thunk and rustle. Curled-up sheets of Bristol board sprung out from nests of bank statements. I kept myself entertained by cross-referencing the lies I'd told her against things I'd said in passing. When no discrepancies suggested themselves, I moved on to wondering what this inheritance might be. Some heirloom already thick with the grease of my caresses, like the Lalique vase? Money? The opportunity to sell my work; a place to start my own gallery? The prolonged childhood of my twenties had become grotesque to me and I was not much good at feeding or cleaning up after the actual children.

I continued to practise the rebellions of my adolescence with long expertise but without relish. They say the ringing sound that follows loud music at a concert is the last note of that pitch you'll ever hear again. My ears still buzzed from my early youth, but the dancing had stopped, everyone else had grown up. Other girls hoped for presents from their boyfriends, not their parents. Nor from other people's girlfriends. I was on the tail end of one disastrous dalliance and at the beginning of another. I had not received a card from Amy, nor from Ida. In Mother's eyes, my loneliness was just more proof I should conform. She often described herself as a practical person.

She had found an envelope and was tearing into it with the letter knife. Through the window, I could see snowdrops around the pond and a furtive cat, white against white snow. Its pawprints led in a semicircle from behind the outbuilding where I liked to paint. Not one of ours. I squatted by the little stove to give the fire encouragement with a poker.

The sound of her setting the knife softly onto the leather of the desk called me back over. She had gone to some effort. Today she was in all the splendour of her self-imposed uniform. Coral-pink lips, blue cashmere and pearls. This usually signified bad news. I sat down opposite and drew the envelope towards myself. Inside, it was patterned with red and green Italianate feathers. It contained a cheque for a considerable sum: I would finally be able to go. If I lived abroad I might not even need to work. There were so many things I hadn't seen. I folded the cheque, and was about to slide it into my bra when Mother took my hand and held it down on the desk, with more force than necessary. I did not like the line of her mouth.

'I have something else to give you.'

'Is it advice?'

'No.'

'Is it jewellery?'

I liked to tell myself I had an artist's appreciation for beautiful things. It was more likely that I had learnt from her the habits of mind which had been so much to her advantage. She looked more surprised than she should have done. 'Yes, it is.'

'Is it the tennis bracelet?'

'I told you, you can't have that, you'll lose it.'

'So I won't lose this, whatever it is?'

Her pressure on the top of my hand intensified. Her hand had the shiny feel that older women's do when they neglect the skin in youth only to slather it with cream in middle age. Syringa. Not what I would have chosen. I painted in fingerless gloves to counteract the cold of the shed, but my fingertips felt raw from spilling white spirit on myself while mixing.

'Look at my wrist.'

The silver bracelet she had always worn was so tight the skin around it had whitened and bulged out pinkly on either side. The little garnet eyes of the snake showed red in the firelight, its mouth full of itself.

She said, 'He's yours now.'

'Thanks but I don't want that, it's not my style. Could you let my hand go, please?'

'I don't think you've quite understood. Look at my wrist.'

I'd thought it must have been light reflecting on the metal. The snake appeared to be moving, his scaly neck swelling outwards. Then his jaws opened imperceptibly wider and with a soft click he took in a little more tail. My mother groaned.

Horror is not dissimilar to love, in that all time gets folded in to meet it. You either feel it still in the present or, in remembering, encounter the numbness of your failure to feel it. I knew then that this moment would never fade comfortably into recollection.

'What do you want me to do with it?'

'It's time you had him.'

'What is it? Whatever it is it needs to go, now. Go to a jeweller's and have it sawn off. Why the fuck are you trying to give it to me?'

'I can't . . . get him off. The minute the saw touches him . . . my hand goes with him.'

'What on earth? Why?'

My mother turned slightly, and with her free hand took down the wedding picture from the shelf behind her. She tapped a lacquered nail against the glass, then drew back her hand. I tried to imagine its absence, the white of a joint poking from the stump.

'Look, I'm thinner here than after I had you.' I had seen these photos many times, and listened to a version of that complaint, but I hadn't noticed the awkward angle of her hand holding my father's. The snake was hurting her there too, yet in the picture next to it, of Mother cradling me as a baby a year later, it hung low on her forearm like a bangle. Now it had grown tight a second time

'It's your turn to take him, and pass him on.'

My legs had crossed themselves before I fully comprehended what she meant. Acid mingled with cake in my mouth.

'That's what the cheque is for, isn't it?'

She sat back into her chair and smiled. On the wall to the left of her, a row of her pastels had faded with the light. She'd said she hadn't had the energy to keep on drawing after I'd arrived. In the silence, I wondered whether the things we do to ourselves and to other people to ensure we have the means to make art often deaden our ability even to appreciate it.

'It's time you started thinking seriously about what you are going to do. There are almost no men around here worth mentioning, and those that are have the wrong idea about you.'

'They have precisely the right idea, Mother.'

It writhed again, more noticeably this time. I will admit to being impressed by her resistance to the pain. Though this would not have been the first time she endured it.

'I don't care about your . . . predilections . . . and neither does he.' She was jabbing at the snake now for emphasis. 'It's not as if they've made you happy anyway.'

'It's different for you, you loved Dad.'

'I did, but you can choose who you love. Starting with your choice of social circle.'

'If I had the choice, I wouldn't love at all. Love is just handing someone a piece of yourself you'll never get back and waiting for them to break it.'

She wrinkled the nose I shared with her. 'There's no need to be so dramatic. If it's that bad for you, then do as I ask. Find someone to help you with this and settle down together.'

I succeeded in yanking my hand out from under hers. It felt damp with the desperate sweat of her palm.

'Whatever stupid bargain you've made, you can leave me out of it. I'm cashing this, by the way.'

She raised her arm and shook it, still pointing. 'Do you think I would have chosen this? Do you think my mother chose it? Or hers? I *wanted* you and I would not have chosen this way. I was getting my first real commissions when it happened. But when my mother told me I had no choice, I put my hand out and accepted him. You really are a selfish girl.'

I picked up the letter knife. 'Do not bring that bracelet anywhere near me. You coward. Just because you accepted it so meekly does not mean you get to pass it on.'

'I'm not frightened of you, you look ridiculous. It's blunt. He's going to take my hand off.'

'I won't do it. This is your problem.'

'And whose problem do you suppose the twins will be, if you sit there in judgement and let me die?'

I pictured a lost decade spent wiping up spills, reading over their homework and trying to comfort them when they asked me what happened to their mother. They would never reach the stage I had, where every confidence became leverage, and so they would always miss her.

I looked down at my own right hand, with its callused middle finger from holding a pen and the black and red acrylic stuck under my nails. I rose early each morning to practise drills with a paintbrush. Supposedly being able to draw a perfect circle meant that you were a genius, but also that you had gone quite mad.

'How long would I have between accepting it and it getting that tight?

'It varies . . . probably five years. Your grandmother had seven. You remember the story about Great Aunt Natasha, Granny's twin? How she was working in a field hospital several miles down the line from Granny when the bomb hit? Granny was your age and the first thing she knew of her sister's death was when she felt him loop around her wrist that night. She said he was the coldest thing she ever felt.'

'Didn't she marry her sister's fiancé? That strikes me as pretty cold.'

'It was a different time. He sorts your life out, you know. Forces you to plan and stop wasting time on other pursuits.'

Avoiding Mother's eyes and the stifled condemnation I knew I would see in them, I looked out of the window again. Ida had promised she would come to the shed when night fell, but I knew she wouldn't. The thought of going to see her with the snake around my wrist disgusted me, anyway. Sex made my body the instrument of my defiance, not some compliant vessel for a greater plan. If it was not wholly mine to use, then it wasn't mine at all. If the sudden loss of my right hand didn't kill me, perhaps I could learn to draw again with the left one.

I spread my fingers out on the dark green leather and turned the knife over in my other hand, so the hilt faced her and the blade faced me.

'Fucking do it then.'

She tried not to look too eager, but the faint lines pulled upwards round her eyes. She tugged at the edge of a moth hole in the hem of her jumper.

'Are you sure you're ready? Because it will be too late to complain about it when he's on you.' I could almost hear her bones cracking under the pressure. 'Wait and see how he feels.'

I would not be the one to pass this on. Maybe it would give me five years, even ten before I had to act. But it would end with me.

I folded my lips against each other and said nothing. She took the hilt and started prising at its jaws.

Five years and the money might be enough. I could finish a lot of canvases in that time. It was preferable to raising my grieving sisters and a lifetime of guilt. Perhaps I had already known enough beautiful things. I tried to think only of those as Mother retook my hand in hers. The sunlight on the snow this morning. The smell of a newly cut lemon. The windows of the Sainte-Chapelle. The place where Ida's hair met the nape of her neck. Swimming naked in the Evenlode in spring. I closed my eyes and waited.

It coiled onto my hand. The snake was burn-cold, death-cold, ice-cold. It paused, considering. Pressure as it settled slowly, then tightened in an instant. A sudden crack. And wet release.

Screaming. I was screaming, then I couldn't breathe. Lungs heaving in and out, as if I could exhale the pain. My eyes were open. On the back of my hand, a raw welt where tiny bubbles of blood were starting to emerge, first slowly then quickly. The hand was broken, fingers curled inwards at odd unnatural angles like a claw. I was too afraid to test them. It was gone. It wasn't on my other wrist, nor on either of my mother's. The pain. I clutched my right wrist in my left hand, keening. The noise didn't seem to come from me, I couldn't stop.

'Where is he? Stop making such a fuss and look for him!' My mother ran around the room, peering under the desk and upending the armchairs, scrabbling as if it

87

might be hiding patiently under the rug, scared by the commotion. A bowl of hyacinths lay smashed on the floor, white roots exposed to the air, their scent mingled with wet soil.

'What did you do?'

I got up, unsteady on my feet and cast about for a cloth to stem the blood, then finding none, shoved open the heavy wooden door with my shoulder.

At the end of the hall, I saw a flicker of a silver tail disappearing down the stairs, headed for the twins.

Lipless Grin

One might excuse any father of a bride the odd glass of sherry to steady his nerves. But I wasn't drinking because of the difficulty in giving Bianca away. I stood over the butler sink in my shiny suit, fussing with the bouquet. I doubted they'd wait for us at the church indefinitely. My finger caught on a thorn and I swore. Bernie hadn't been satisfied with the flowers when they'd arrived early this morning, but the car came before she had time to fix the arrangement.

It never showed in photographs. We had plenty displayed in mother-of-pearl frames in the drawing room. Bernie used to request photos for Christmas, complaining how hard it was to find one our daughter liked. She looked tall and womanly in those, with Bernie's reddish hair and perfect teeth. But her eyes were from my side of the family, more similar to poor cousin Annabel's. Bernie wasn't sure why she'd insisted on an old-fashioned dress – I was told it covered her from wrist to throat. I wondered if she'd made such a concealing choice in case she collapsed into sludge on crossing the threshold.

She was eleven when the rot set in. At that time I liked to go around the local chemist's at weekends and check that the products whose accounts I managed were in pride of place. Bianca would come with me and I'd buy the flavoured pastilles that Bernie never allowed her. She was always withdrawn at home, but talked away at me on those afternoons about pet cats and castles and other storybook nonsense. Sometimes I'd buy her cheap cosmetics if she promised to be quiet.

One Sunday, I had been double-checking what we'd managed to keep off the label of a firming cream when the patter stopped. I had hoped they would expand that range next year and I could delegate the powdered-milk account. Nobody had ever been able to prove the stuff caused malnutrition and prematurely loosened baby teeth, but being in charge of it was a headache.

These contemplations led me to wonder whether all Bianca's teeth could be out yet. She wasn't in the shop. I made two circuits, trying not to panic. I checked behind all the cardboard displays of the round-arsed women whom we always had to imply were French. I burst outside, still holding the cream and tore round the corner. Little Bianca was standing halfway up the street, weeping and bleeding from the nose. She was crying so hard the blood started coming out of her mouth as well and frothing up. She buried her face in my chest. Bianca had followed a man in an identical blue tweed coat out of the chemist, thinking he was me. She told me he'd said some things to her that she hadn't understood and she ran back towards the shop, but couldn't remember where exactly the shop was. We agreed that telling Bernie would only agitate her and I threw away my shirt when I couldn't get the stain out.

She was even quieter in the weeks after that, and so pale she looked almost blue. Bernie complained she held herself stiffly, even when embraced. Around this time, an old friend let me know I had been nominated for an industry award. I was away a lot, talking to the right people at parties and going on sales visits overseas. Bernie was already annoyed with me for working too much. If I confessed, I'd never stop hearing about it.

On my visits home, I couldn't help but notice Bianca was getting quite tubby. She mostly stayed in her room, even on the occasions I was back in time to kiss her goodnight. I tried talking to Bernie about it — wasn't she worried our daughter would get bullied? I needed my family to be presentable. Bianca had always looked younger than she was, I was so proud of her ability to enchant my colleagues when they visited.

'Can't you make her exercise? Are you feeding her lots of junk?'

Apparently, she barely ate at all, and complained of always feeling cold when told to go outside and run around. I thought Bernie was being soft, but hinting at this would get me another lecture. As if I could always be at home *and* working to pay for the girls at once.

'Really, it looks more like bloat than fat. With any luck it will go away as her body changes.' With these words, Bernie closed the conversation.

When I had time, I would bring back little gifts for Bianca, to try and cheer her up. A bit of effort would do her good. But no matter how luxurious the products I took home for her were, I would always find them back in my study, seals unbroken.

My cousin Annabel at her age was so sweet and polite. Our parents shared a little house on the coast where we played together every summer. They thought she would survive the fever, though it took her fingers and toes. Advanced up joint by joint until she was only a torso, delirious. I wasn't meant to hear these details, nor my mother's description of her flesh, boiled red and mottled black as Annabel's limbs gave way. The house was sold, we never visited again.

One morning, I was composing an invitation to my assistant to resign, while pretending to listen to Bernie. She'd been so promising, really the kind of face we could see in the boardroom one day. But she found a report on the milk powder and wouldn't stop asking me about it. I'd pointed out to her that our rival would have sold the stuff if we hadn't, but it was becoming obvious she was in the wrong field. I cast a distracted eye across the table, past the centrepiece to Bianca's hand, scraping the spoon round and round her half-filled bowl. Just by her hand rested something white, I assumed it was a petal from the centrepiece until it moved.

I felt the milk turn in my mouth as I stared at it. Bernie carried on talking, Bianca's head was bent down. As I tried to catch her gaze, another one fell out of her loose auburn hair to join the first maggot on the table. Coming back to myself, I slammed my mug down on the pair of them. Bernie was furious.

'What's wrong with you? If you really don't want to get the garden repaved, you could just tell me like a civilised human being. We've broken two mugs and a wineglass this month alone.'

I was going to miss my train. As I was making my excuses, Bianca finally looked up. I was pleased to see she was less plump than before, though her face looked strange, both squashed and slack, as if she had too much skin.

Not long afterwards, the house became filled with an odour not unlike urine, but with a sweet overtone and strangely familiar. Bernie claimed she couldn't smell a thing. It became increasingly difficult to know what I should say to Bianca. She came downstairs dressed up to go out and turned to the little oval mirror by the door to add some finishing touches. She brushed some white dust from off her shoulders, adjusted a fingernail. She must have seen my reflection watching her as she grabbed a peeling section near the top of her brow and yanked it down, exposing the livid flesh underneath. The white of her smile was bright within her taut grey mouth.

I started looking for excuses to stay late and took Bernie on breaks to various spas, telling her she deserved some rest. She was still as slender as a girl, but not without effort. If only our daughter could have retained some of her mother's charm.

Eventually, enough time passed that Bianca could be sent away to study in another city. I mostly heard about her from Bernie. We were very proud of her achievements. The smell died down a little.

At the height of summer a few years later, I left work early one Friday afternoon. It was neither Christmas nor Easter, but there were what looked like a pair of Bianca's sandals in the rack and some large brogues. She'd met a young man, and they were living together. Supposedly, Bianca had always wanted to get married in our little local church and was wondering if we could host the wedding breakfast afterwards. I looked into her shrivelled eye sockets and it was all I could do not to refuse.

Bernie was thrilled with Ed, he was such a gentleman, with a good job and so caring towards our daughter. His family would be coming all the way from Virginia for the ceremony, though we wouldn't be expected to put them up. Bianca stretched an arm round Ed. Her hand, with its taut and gummy skin, nearly touched my shoulder.

She and Bernie went upstairs to look at pictures of potential dresses. I tried to make conversation, asking Ed if he'd seen any billboards from our new razor campaign on the drive up. He turned his empty glass in semicircles on the table, turning the coaster with it.

'Aren't you going to give me your blessing?'

He waited for my response, but I could hardly warn him. He lived with the creature for whom I felt such revulsion and had not noticed. Perhaps he did notice and liked it.

I studied him in the lamplight, picked over his wide jaw and dark hair swept to one side. An impulsive face. Not someone I would hurry to employ.

He asked again, 'Nothing? Not even a few friendly words? I suppose I should have expected this. She's told me all about you.'

He looked as if he would say more, but then lowered his high white forehead and swept out, turning off the light as he went. I sat in the dark for a long time, trying to breathe through my mouth. Since that night, he and Bianca had been coming and going without giving word, and the quality of my work suffered. They were just down the hall, in her childhood bedroom. This wedding was ruining my sleep. I sat waiting with the roses and looked forward to it all being over.

I heard Bianca's tread in the corridor upstairs. She was walking down carefully, a thick veil already covering her face. Her hand was concealed in a lace glove, and she briefly rested it on mine as she came down the last few steps. My palm still stung from the place where the thorn went in. We went together to the car. I was preparing to roll down the windows as I always did when alone with her, but all I could smell were the flowers. I must have been rougher than I thought, for them to release so much scent.

I was cold in my suit inside the church, despite the sun shining outside. Glad to pass her over to Ed, I went to sit by my wife, trying not to look like I was in a hurry. The service wore on; I wanted to look away from Ed kissing his bride, but found I couldn't. As she pulled back the veil, I understood why it had taken her so long to get ready. People often say that brides are radiant, but they mean something else entirely. I couldn't be sure if I was crying from the pain in my hand, or the stark beauty of her bare skull in the light from above.

Hags

I should have just torn my face off and started again, it wasn't sitting right. I'd slicked red over my lips, traced my lashline in black — and ping! — all ruined by my phone as my startled hand jerked the liner upwards. But my skin grew back slowly when I hadn't fed in a fortnight and I'd promised Erin I wouldn't be late.

I sighed, swiped cold cream over my lids and started again. Ping! The nuisance machine was enough to make me long for the days when a breviary and a dagger were the only props I needed.

Hekla: doors at midnight, don't bail on us

Hekla: it'll be the last time for a while xx

They must have been caught up in the tourist rush, the ones who only came to Adversary to say they'd been and usually left after the intro performances gave way to the main entertainment. Yes to acrobats, no to fleshhooks. It's not like they weren't warned; every edgy magazine in London had commissioned an identical article, sending a rookie in to gawk, when they were able to get tickets. The rookies always professed astonishment, then made it clear they hadn't partaken in the fun. At least photographers were banned, they scared off my prey. Adversary never happened in the same place twice – private homes, cavernous gay saunas, warehouses in suburban business parks all played host. It never got shut down. Erin had run the numbers once and realised someone must be subsidising our festivities, but we'd never found out who.

Finally the flicks went right, two grandiose black swoops straining towards my ponytail, which was pulled up high and playfully braided into nine dark strands. Ishi always said I was overcompensating. That wasn't quite it – for as long as I had to wear this silly body, I might as well gesture at its fakeness. I loved hiding in plain sight, whereas they had struggled to stay peaceably in any place for long. One of so many ways our methods differed. That said, I'd only learnt not to party with my wings out after brushing past a lit cigarette and getting caught in an interminable discussion with two SFX technicians about the most flame-resistant silicone blends.

I called myself a cab and leant out of the window to wait for its arrival near my sublet of a sublet. Broken glass glittered in a spray around the overflowing bins, while unseen birds sang to the orange glow of a streetlamp. I'd chosen grottily and chosen well. It was still just about possible to remain minimally involved with bureaucracy, but every decade it got harder. I hadn't stolen anyone's identity in a while, I was sorely out of practice thanks to a self-perpetuating desire to stay put. It was getting to be that time again. I had to contend with the pain of parting or the dullness of accompanying my favourite humans through the latter halves of their brief lives with my own plausible imitation of ageing.

The cab deposited me near Marble Arch, in front of a luxury hotel so stodgy that its cachet must have ceased to register with the intended clientele. And now Adversary was here. The doorman took my password with white-gloved disgust.

'It's in the penthouse, madam, suite 77.'

After a second exchange of passwords at the threshold, I slunk my way through the glittery, beharnessed throng, peering over revellers' heads in search of Erin. At six foot tall and elegantly draped with blues and greens, she was always easy to spot in a crowd. Beside her Hekla, butch and handsomely impish, one arm curled round her rounded belly, protecting its contents from the crowd. I tasted a topnote of irritation, laid over the deep contentment that usually emanated from both of them. I'd drained these two dry of any essence that could sustain me. My hunger had long been transmuted into deep affection, both for them individually and for their bond. I'd brushed up against so many bad relationships, this one was rare.

'Finally, I can have my one drink.' Hekla swiped three bellinis from the open bar. '*Skál!*'

Erin asked 'Do you want to catch any of the performances, Asta? We watched a man slide a skewer through both cheeks earlier and encourage the crowd to throw marshmallows for him to catch.'

'I told you, he was using old holes, I saw the same thing in Stockholm once.'

'Don't you dare change, either of you.' I raised my glass in a little toast.

Hekla snorted. 'I wouldn't know how. Anyway, once the baby has arrived we'll have to be much more focussed with our partying because it will happen less often.'

The sentence I'd known was coming but had avoided hearing until now. Erin and Hekla's encroaching motherhood had set something off inside me, like a great wave stirred into life by the rumbling of a volcano on the shore. I had no wish to contemplate the wreckage.

'Do you know . . .?' I tried counting backward in my head and gave up. I didn't operate in weeks.

'Probably not for another month. It's like wandering around with a little bomb. Hopefully not tonight.'

Erin addedd, 'Though that would make a great origin story, when they're old enough to hear it.'

'Let's go to the other room,' I said.

We made our way past the crowd who had gathered to watch as a short-haired woman covered in spiralling scarifications deposited an enormous boa constrictor onto the back of another bound figure suspended by shibari ropes from rings in the ceiling. The boa raised its fawn-coloured head to watch me as I left. *Hello friend.*

The vast lounge area was strewn with assorted queers, vaping on chaises longues, throwing the leftover marshmallows at each other and cavorting on the red-sheeted beds dotted throughout the space. The imploring, keening sound of a woman's voice accompanying a sitar thrummed over twining bodies in the low light. Towards the back was an area partly concealed by standing screens, patterned with a vast skeleton menacing two samurai, from behind which the sounds of slapping and grunting occasionally issued.

Through a gap in the screens, I saw a slender man strapped upside down to a leather Catherine wheel while another fastened clothes pegs to every spare inch of his bruised skin. Two high femmes with long blue tresses were weaving green ribbons in a corset pattern around the needles they'd inserted into a third girl's back. The air shimmered with excess, aureate emotion. I darted out my tongue for a moment, sampled excitement, uncertainty, lust and joy. Pleasant enough, but not what I was looking for. Erin went to beg a cushion from one of the other groups for Hekla to sit on. As we were settling ourselves, I spotted someone I remembered dimly from last year, her face now framed by long blonde hair, shoulders unclenched. She caught my eye and smiled, twinkled her fingers and turned back to her conversation.

'Is that . . .?' Erin had been observing.

'Yeah, I met her at that party last year under the arches, the one with the fire eaters. She looked a little different then.'

Erin rolled her eyes. 'What is it with you and newly out girls? You know what, next time you go home with someone, give her my number instead of yours, so I can add her to one of my trans support chats.'

I laughed and made an empty-handed shrug. It was hardly news to me that Erin was extremely sharp, but this was a clue to my real nature I'd rather she not possess.

Hekla said, 'Give her a break, half the people in here are my exes or my exes' exes.'

'We all know about you, darling. You came on your long-boat all the way from Hlíðarendi to ravish our womenfolk.' Erin leant in for a kiss, hand caressing to Hekla's belly.

'And to be ravished by them, as the mood takes me,' Hekla smirked.

Neither of them knew exactly how right Erin was – a long, long while ago I'd had some dealings with an ancestor of Hekla's, a rather slippery character but a bold seafarer. I liked to check in on certain lines, see the traits and mannerisms I missed so much stretch implausibly across the generations. It made me mourn my old friends less, when they were under earth and I still walked this world alone.

As Erin and Hekla sank deeper into one another, I continued to scan the room, feeling increasingly faint. There must be someone here who needed me, and who in turn had what I needed. When I'd first emerged, I'd been able to eat anything from anyone. It had taken centuries to refine my tastes and then my body started to reject most flavours of vital essence. The foolish warlock who'd summoned me had kept me submerged up to the neck in a pool of holy water he'd hidden under a remote outhouse. The water did nothing, but the sigils he'd carved into the surrounding rocks took a few days to undo. Once I'd slipped my bonds, I reduced him to a heap of sentient ash and plundered his library, teaching myself the human tongue as I went. He'd planned on interrogating me about the 'nether realms', as if I could remember anything. Doorways often warped bodies and wiped minds near-clean. If I had one complaint about this plane it was that making openings in and out of it was far too easy for the average bumbler; I'd met others of my kind who had been pulled through in a similarly abrupt fashion. Or they left on a whim and were never heard from again. *Oh Ishi, where are you now? What sulphurous sky burnishes your wings, what molten earth warms you with its flaming gusts?*

A tap on my left shoulder. 'Excuse me? Is that a split tongue?' I turned, sensing as I did so that here at last might be my prey. My interlocutor was small and shy, cowering a little as if she hadn't expected me to answer. Her choppy homemade haircut suggested a lack of anyone to help her.

'It is.' I poked it out again, flexing one part then the other before quickly withdrawing. It was the only aspect of this form I couldn't change.

'Didn't it hurt terribly?' Since humans had started doing this to themselves I'd had versions of the question more and more. I used to tell people that I'd lost a bet.

'I wouldn't say so. Were you thinking of getting one?' She settled herself next to me in the space vacated by Erin and Hekla, who had somehow acquired a third person mid-makeout and were all heading towards the screened area hand in hand, stepping high over other groups writhing on the carpet.

'I'd never dare. It looks cool though.' She looked away. I touched her jawline softly with one finger and raised her head to look at me.

'Would you like to find out how it feels?' I pulled her in, searching, fingertips sprouting hair-fine hooks dripping with elixir in anticipation. Here was anxiety, eagerness and yes, the dark, acrid reservoir of shame I craved. Most delicious of the vital essences. This one should sustain me for a while.

'Not bad, hm?'

Blushing, she came back for more, then pulled away.

'Should we . . . go over there?' She pointed towards the screens. Even in this secret place, surrounded by those whose desires placed them beyond the protection of the law, I could not make my own needs known.

'I don't like to go too far in public, but if you want to take me home I should probably say goodbye to some people. Did you come with anyone?'

She shook her head. 'We can leave now.'

'Wait here.' I darted over to the back, and craned my neck round. They'd found two dark wooden thrones, side by side. Hekla sat in one and her new friend in the other. Erin was already wrist deep in both of them, her shoulders stacked with legs, the vegvísir Hekla had tattooed onto Erin's back glistening with sweat.

'Guys, I'm off, you know the drill.'

Hekla groaned, 'Really, you're such a prude, you just got here . . . ohhh – just a bit to the left, Erin – OK well, have fun, be safe.'

'I know, I'm sorry! Still great to see you, though.' I blew her a kiss. Their new friend winked at me and waved.

Erin turned her head and grinned. 'I'd wave you goodbye too, but I'm a little busy right now. Come over for dinner next week if we're not in hospital and tell us all about them.'

I managed to keep it together until I'd reached the girl's bedroom, though I was so starving that it was a struggle not to vomit up the little taste I'd already had. She kept cuddling up to me in the cab as I tried to hold myself primly away. I twitched and shifted, trying to disguise the sinews jabbing up beneath my skin and threatening to break this form apart. *Don't make me kill you and the driver.* She asked several times if I was drunk and then if I was sure it would be OK, disappointment and responsibility warring in her tone. With some effort, I put my hands over hers, to administer a preliminary dose of calming elixir. I hated feeding when they were nervous.

Her room was spare, a narrow queen bed with a poster for *Heavenly Creatures* framed above it and a rail of frothy dresses with the tags still on. Battered diaries were stacked in a pile and a stained blind covered the window.

She peeled off her clothes and tried to start on mine. I pinned her to the bed by her wrists, seeing in her eyes the tell-tale look of release.

'I'll be taking things from here, if you don't mind.'

She smiled and nodded and I set to work.

It is a curious thing about humans that if they are properly enjoying themselves, they don't really care when you have more limbs than you ought to or notice the shadow of wings spotlit against a wall. The shame drained out and down my gullet in long bittersweet spurts, sometimes accompanied by overlays of memory. A child standing alone in a city park at dusk, droplets of blood dried into a pair of jeans, a pitch-dark room with the sensation of small, soft hands finding their way into a sleeping bag. It was rich and plentiful, with notes of rage and fear that lent it additional savour. I would be returning here. If I'd lain with someone once, I could send myself back in dreams, to polish off the supply. From the comfort of my sandbath at home, I folded reality a little to superimpose myself in the room, crouched on chests and kissed eyelids, gorging myself. They didn't need it and I did. I tried to make the process as painless as possible, leaving only the vaguest sense of a presence.

Sated for the moment, I made sure to finish her off. She cried out and clung to me, then, moments later, asked, 'Is there nothing I can do for you?'

'You've done more than enough. I'm getting a little tired now.' And with a last kiss, I gave her enough elixir to bring on a sweet and dreamless sleep.

Skin shucked off and draped over the door, I rolled around my tank, kicking up iridescent clouds of silica and coiling every which way to get the cramps out. I was poised to start playing a slideshow of close-ups from Bosch paintings over the projector when my phone went off next door and I had to crawl out of the boxroom. The closet I'd adapted wasn't visible to human guests because I'd pinched reality and tied it off in a pouch, though they did tend to get disorientated in the hallway. Erin had texted to let me know she was planning a 'final final hurrah' and to keep next Friday free. I tried and failed to avoid the melancholy that accompanied a full stomach. Ishi's absence was most palpable when I had no other needs to occupy myself with. We'd always shared this world together – they came through the door hooked into my flank like a sweet little burr and by the time I'd noticed them, they'd burrowed all the way inside. Ishi grew within me those first few years, gaining strength as I ate for two. I used to lie in piles of dead villagers and hear Ishi's heart beating in rhythm with my own as I watched the carrion circling overhead. Only in the last phase, when my belly became distended and they kept sending out feelers to try and take over my limbs did I get impatient and tear them free. Full grown, they flew off immediately, dripping with essence, back muscles rippling and gleaming in the sun. We didn't meet again until decades later in Russia, when I came across them impersonating a priest, ranting about pictures of the devil hidden under icons and riling the crowd into a frenzy. Ishi made the rabble barge into churches to throw stones and scream wild accusations. I had recently stolen the life of a rich nobleman and I got into the spirit of the jape, confronting them and insisting that this was all a ploy to desecrate images of the Virgin. It ended with me having my men arrest Ishi and drag them to my dacha. We didn't leave for weeks. Biting, piercing, breaking sinews, healing to do it all again. We passed pain back and forth between us like language. A different order of magnitude to the dalliances human bodies could withstand. We tore through so many serfs during snack breaks we had to bury the estate under a landslide.

It wasn't all romance – we got annoyed with each other easily and often spent years apart. Back then, it was important to me to have a project, like collecting miniatures or rigging elections, and Ishi preferred wreaking havoc. They loved surprises. One of their favourite ways to let me know they were thinking about me was to send an individual they'd drained of all resistance to infiltrate my schemes, then spontaneously start a massacre. After one such occasion, I pulled Ishi's head off and put it in a box on top of their wardrobe with eyeholes cut out so they could watch me seduce their favourite pet. Ishi regenerated in such a fury they unhinged their jaw and swallowed me whole. Nestled in the warm dark of Ishi's stomach, with the essence they'd drained out of various people swirling around me, I drifted off. I knew they'd get bored and let me out eventually. When we hunted together, we were sleek, invincible, perfectly attuned to the other's next move. I didn't have to worry when Ishi was gone, because they always came back. I still hoped they would.

It was time to go to the Wallace Collection. I folded my feelers in and tucked my wings tight, growing a fine layer of reflective scales to hold everything in place before skin and hair went over the top. A little spritz of perfume. There were a surprising number of us on the tube, ever since there'd been a tube to ride on. Great clay fellows riding glumly into the centre on errands, wraiths clinging to their unwitting hosts, the occasional lost fae. We minded our own business, and it was generally understood that no one should be hunting in a place so infested with CCTV. I got off at Baker Street and sped through the human hordes out ambling in the June sunshine. I had a bar shift starting in a couple of hours and I hadn't quite got to grips with new gin selection yet. As I reached the museum and rushed up the stairs, a throng of ormolu clocks began striking three in sequence throughout the building. I'd amassed and squandered far better art collections in my time, but this one held the only known picture of Ishi. Wearing a dainty white dress and dun turban, a bag of strawberries clutched to their stomach, they glared out of the frame with dark and knowing eyes. The portrait was painted at the beginning of our extended disagreement about the proper treatment of humans – I'd begun to lose interest in slaughter and spent most of my time in molly houses, siphoning off my friends' overflowing shame and carousing together. I'd found that I preferred what they gave me freely to anything I could take by force. As a compromise, Ishi walked the streets in the guise of an abandoned child, devouring those who attempted to purchase more than fruit. They had loved me and they had really tried, the painting was proof.

I felt for the puckered knot in the air beside the frame and slowly pushed in a fingertip at a time, squeezing myself gradually into the cache. I made one for every place I lived – the human memories that were a by-product of my feeding supply got mixed up with my own and needed to be milked out at regular intervals. Caches were also a good place to keep languages I wasn't using and keepsakes of the friends I'd lost. Rows of haphazardly labelled vials: Yiddish grammar; Southwark Stews 1599, Margery F; Piers Gaveston misc; Principles of Millinery. A jacquard silk doublet and breeches bestowed on me by a dashing privateer. A broken masonry gargoyle blown off St Ethelreda's during the Blitz stood guard over a pile of letters written in different hands, playbills and flyers for the Vauxhall Pleasure Gardens. Soon I'd need to collate and print off all the messages from Erin and Hekla for a folder here. I couldn't stay. It hurt too much to watch my friends grow old. And yet, I hated manufacturing disagreements or inflicting grief through faking my own death. *What if I just told them?* The idea was stupid, they'd never believe me and if they did, they'd be appalled. They'd both been so frank with me about their own hopes and disappointments, Erin's rift with her family and Hekla's arrest after vandalising a police car during a protest. They'd met while working at a refugee camp in Lebanon before Erin's transition and dedicated their lives

110

to helping others. I'd seldom seen either of them pass a beggar without opening her purse. How could I explain to the gentlest people I knew that I used to torment nuns and stake Ottoman armies for entertainment? That, for all my effort to be good, I mostly fed by sleights of hand? They'd never let me near the baby.

Work went quickly, we'd revamped the menu and taken a vast order of luxury garnishes. I ladled squidgy cherries out of the jar to ram on golden skewers and snuck tiny spoonfuls of peaty amber whisky to match it with the correct spring water. Nothing but the best for visitors to Birch Tower. My favourite regulars got a little dash of elixir to top off their drinks. I seldom hunted at work any more, tempting as it often was. In my last job, one patron I'd slipped my number to had somehow intuited whose fault it was he no longer felt shame when forced to kiss away the accumulated dirt from women's shoes and waited outside one night to confront me for ruining the pleasure of his abjection. I had chosen what I thought least likely to wound through its removal, but there were still so many who needed what I craved.

Mostly I just churned out glass after glass of top-shelf classics for the suits and made fruity concoctions sprinkled with gold leaf for their wives and mistresses. The real draw of the job was wiping down tables after closing, when I could look out across the dark city from the fiftieth floor, sparkling like an upended box of gems and dream of flying over it again. I missed soaring uninterrupted by the police or military so much it felt like a piercing ache in my wing buds.

Friday night rolled around sooner than expected and Erin and Hekla's dented navy panel van drew up outside my door at nine pm sharp.

'Get in loser, we're going witching,' Hekla yelled out of the driver's side window. I got in the back with Erin and Maribel, who I'd had a couple of dates with years ago and who now ran a small Santería shop in Peckham. An attractive woman with a frohawk and lots of silver earrings sat shotgun.

Erin said, 'Ola, this is Asta, she's an old friend of ours. You two are both into river swimming and arthouse films. Ola works in music production.' Ola turned to stare at me, unblinking.

'Hi, Ola! Pleased to meet you ... Is this some sort of sabbat?' I'd forgotten they were into this, Hekla had mentioned going to álfablóts at home but nothing quite like this.

'You could say that. Maribel talked me into it and I thought I might as well, since it's midsummer.' Ola reached round to rifle through the CD cases scattered on the floor between sunflower-patterned beanbags and crumbling sticks of the incense Erin liked.

'Where are we going, exactly?'

Hekla chipped in. 'Just a place I know. It's good there, I've been before.'

Ola leant forward and shoved a disc into the CD player, filling the van with house music. She didn't seem inclined to keep the conversation going. Maribel began telling a long story about picketing a coal mine in Germany and I had a little nap. With the new rush of energy from my hookup after Adversary, I'd called in for three double shifts and was now regretting it. I'd been back to the girl twice now, with diminishing returns – I had to leave just enough shame to keep her from the madhouse. I'd found it was imperative to let my prey retain at least the dregs, or else they lost all self-preservation and forgot the complicated rules humans had invented for one another. Often the ones with the most plentiful supply had the greatest number of rules to bind them, so I'd developed taking just the right amount into a fine art. The last time, I'd been sitting beside her, rootling and tugging the last of my portion loose when she sat up and asked who was there. Her finger was already on the light switch by the time I'd ricocheted back home.

I woke a couple of hours later and immediately knew something wasn't right. The van was parked in a copse and it was still twilight outside. The atmosphere hummed and bulged, throbbing with loose energy. Hekla had managed to choose a spot for her sabbat where reality was very thin. She led us through the trees to an open plain where a circle of grey stones stood tall above the grass. The air shimmered with heat and I smelt smoke where none was to be seen. Fear started building in my chest, and I doubled over wheezing with a coughing fit.

Ola, wrapped in a thick yellow shawl, looked from me to the hulking, mossy rocks and back with increasing suspicion. How much could she see of what I was seeing? Some humans were more sensitive than others, though perhaps she was just sleepy.

'Asta, what's wrong? Who's got the thermos?' Erin was rubbing my back and holding my hair away out of my face. She poured out a cupful of steaming black coffee for me, infused with cinnamon and muscovado sugar.

'I . . . I . . . don't think we should be doing this.'

She straightened up. 'You're not a Christian, are you? You never said.'

'No, but . . .' How could I explain to her that I could feel vast, unidentifiable presences swimming nearby? That if anyone managed to open the smallest rift there was a good chance all of them would spend the rest of eternity being repeatedly flayed and feasted on?

Hekla said, 'It'll be fine, we're just celebrating the turning of the year. It's nothing malicious.'

I considered blasting them all with elixir and driving the van straight home, but that would leave too many questions unanswered. My only hope was sabotage.

'Come on, get in before the light goes.' Erin was casting a circle of salt widdershins around the stones. A little before she reached the point she'd started at, she beckoned us all inside then scattered the rest on the ground to mark the join, which I checked furtively, tracing the most repellent sigil I could think of into the earth with my toe nearby. We stood, holding hands, and without anyone instructing us, we began to move round and round, humming tunelessly, speed tempered only by Hekla's cargo. Little by little I noticed Ola's eyes turning back into her head, whites shining in the greenish dusk, before she began to chant in an entirely different voice than any I'd heard her use that night, rasping and whispering, with odd snatches of song. I'd left my Yoruba in the Lagos cache and not knowing what she said or who she was saying it to only panicked me more. If she had the powers I thought she might, it was small wonder she hadn't warmed to this place. Below us, a rumble, something turning, reality growing thinner by the minute. I saw the pupil of a giant eye roll beneath our feet and fix us with its curious gaze. We spun faster and a mist rose round the stones, shadows surging forward within it. Bristling tongues darted out, probing for the backs of our legs. I screamed and simulated tripping, landing with deliberate awkwardness to gash open my forearm with a talon as I fell. I could have fixed it in moments, but I didn't.

The silence in the van had barely thawed by the time we'd driven to UCH and the total lack of parking near A&E had not helped much. I'd apologised profusely to everyone for my clumsiness and cutting short the sabbat. Ola muttered under her breath that it was probably for the best. When Erin asked if she'd ever gone into a trance like that before, she said she hadn't and seemed embarrassed. I suspected someone must have tipped her off while we were in the circle, since now she wouldn't even meet my gaze. Ishi had often frolicked along the Osun river and said that its priestesses were not easily deceived. Hopefully she might be able to convince the others they should never return to the stones. Erin and Hekla tried to insist on going into the hospital with me but I could see they were drooping with exhaustion and guilt. Maribel kept saying 'I checked the ground for bottles, I don't understand what happened.' After they'd driven off, I waited in the lobby for ten minutes until I was certain the coast was clear, then found a nearby toilet to pinch the wound shut. If I went to buy some plasters in the morning, no one would be able to tell I'd healed.

Ishi would have found the whole thing ridiculous, assuming that they hadn't been there watching and laughing throughout. I didn't know which Hell dimension they were in – the gate at Derweze was very unstable, shifting orientation frequently and spitting out members of our kind from different planes. Of those who had retained some memory, not a single account matched the others that I'd heard. The night before Ishi made the dive, they tried to convince me to accompany them. We were floating in a storm cloud over Lake Baikal, wings beating together in the soft grey static. Electricity crackled along our intertwined limbs as lightning shot down into the water. Both of us loved the scent of ozone.

'Don't you want to go on an adventure? I'm so bored, it's been over fifty years and they haven't thought of any new atrocities, just the same ones with a slightly different spin each time.'

'There's more to do than carnage, try branching out a bit. The other day I found an underwater cavern full of crates and I'm pretty sure the Amber Room is in those.'

'Oh, you found that? I put that there for you, I wondered when you'd get to it.'

I leant in for a kiss, shooting barbed tendrils under their skin to draw them even closer. They put out a stinger and hovered it menacingly above my head.

'Stop trying to distract me. Will you come or not?'

'I like it here. I have my friends, I go on trips and I have you.'

'You're always sad because your pets are dying and you don't hunt properly any more. You used to be fun.'

'But what about all your caches? If you leave, you'll forget everything.' Thunder clapped around us and light flashed, illuminating their silvery scales. I worried that my heart would burst and Ishi would just let me tumble into the icy depths below.

'I'll make new ones. And if we go through at the same time, we might fuse, you'd like that.'

'But I love you because you *aren't* me. This world is big enough for both of us to wander and small enough to meet again. What if we get ripped apart by the slipstream and end up in different planes?'

'I have to go, Asta. I've already decided.'

We'd made our choices and I had never been certain whether mine was wrong. Walking back from the hospital through the rush of early dawn, I wrestled again with the mad urge to confide in Erin and Hekla. They were careful not to press me too hard for the reason I moved through parties like Adversary and Plinth mainly as a spectator and yet kept coming along with them. They knew how to keep secrets when it mattered. I couldn't burden them with this, could I? I was not the woman they believed me to be, indeed I was no woman at all, I was only like this because most humans needed me to pick one or the other. Perhaps Ola had already told them how dangerous I was and they were packing up the house to flee.

The breeze over Regent's Canal blew cold, mildewy air over my face as I followed its current homewards. Rather than turning left onto the high street, I took a sharp right through the square, and then another right, onto a quiet residential street lined with sycamores. At number 34, the front garden was filled with blue ceramic pots of herbs and cherry tomatoes, while pea plants twisted up bamboo supports towards the rising sun. We'd planted them together in April and Hekla had given me a pot of my own to take away. She had only just begun showing then, but Erin was already darting forward to save her the strain of bending as we dug in the gravelly earth, hoping to coax life from such unpromising soil. I'd watched them sitting on the low wooden bench, as the magnolia tree bloomed above them, Hekla clasping Erin's hand and kissing her cheek as they talked about their shared future. Now, I stood looking up at the house as the light turned from teal to apricot, reaching blindly forward in time as I wondered what sort of person their child would grow to be. Might there be some small role for me yet, if ageless I remained?

Their blue-painted door should hardly have been as daunting as Derweze, but this was still a gamble and whatever I won or lost, the outcome was inevitably change.

I beat on the knocker and Erin answered in surprise, hair still tousled from the scant hours of sleep she'd managed to snatch since I'd seen her last.

'Come in! Come and have a cup of tea, we've been so worried.' She came forward to embrace me.

'I know it's very early, but there's something I have to tell you.'

The Bequest

One up and two down, the tiny collection of warren-like rooms could scarcely be classified as a house, but Great Aunt Ruth had always referred to it as such and had managed to cram it with enough possessions to fill somewhere three times the size. She wasn't even our great aunt, but an older relative of our grandmother's, who had fled here during the war and promptly jilted the man she'd been brought over to marry. We cousins were to be allowed our pick of her things.

This was assuming we could get at them under the moth-eaten blankets and tchotchkes balanced as precariously as if they were rudimentary booby traps. Aaron had already been and gone, taking only a coveted blue ceramic bowl from which we'd been served aniseed-flavoured candies on special occasions. Naomi was six months pregnant and couldn't be bothered. After our visit, the worst of the cleaning was to be done by professionals – my father had insisted on it, to my aunt's chagrin. Johnny collected me and Sasha in his bright blue Fiat, an eighteenth-birthday gift we had envied at the time, and instructed me to fold myself up in order to fit in the back.

For company, I had a half-empty packet of Camels, a *Gray's Anatomy* with the cover torn off and a variety of expensive-looking camping flasks. I consoled myself with the thought that if anyone had inherited Ruth's possessive tendencies it was definitely him.

'How are we going to take anything back with us in this tiny clown car? You, me and Miri barely fit in it now.' Sasha was a month and a half older than Johnny and had always taken pains not to let him forget it.

He said, 'Stop twiddling the radio, you're just making it static. If we find anything worth having, we can stick a note to it and try to drag it into the hall for the van men.'

Sasha kept twiddling. I reached forward and turned the radio off.

If I talked, there was a very real chance that I might vomit. The inside of my head felt crunchy. Last night I'd reached the stage of drunkenness where I'd declared to everyone that I wasn't drunk at all and then promptly tripped over a coffee table. My shin had bruised so deeply there was no mark to show what had occurred. My phone screen stayed stubbornly blank, I had no new texts.

Sasha turned to Johnny and said, 'You really didn't ever visit, did you? The hall's full of old ladders and that broken rocking horse you pulled over with a cat-leash when you were seven.'

'Funnily enough, no, I've been in Jo'burg learning how to plug gunshot wounds. She was ninety-eight, she could have gone any time the past two decades.'

I looked at my phone again. Lucy had promised me she'd get better about replying to messages, but after a month of contrite attentiveness it was just the same, a yes–no question could take her three days to answer, and a statement without a question mark might languish up to a week, supposedly unread. I was permanently tensed for the little ping that would show she had remembered my existence.

Johnny gave the indicator a cursory flick as we turned off onto a narrow residential street and said, 'If either of you get peckish, you must try some of my mother's wedding cake, I'm told it's still in the freezer. Even tastier with the aerosol whipped cream, best before 1995.'

Sasha groaned in disgust then retrieved her lip balm for a third application since getting in the car. She hated for anyone to acknowledge the scale of Ruth's hoarding, which was probably how she'd managed to keep returning well into adulthood.

Lucy had surprised me with an offer to come and help, but her inevitable reaction to the house would hurt Sasha too much and I'd fumbled my excuses, so no texts for me.

The house smelt like chamomile tea, dust and cat urine. The cats were nowhere to be seen, though I feared turning up a desiccated specimen under all the piles of *National Geographic*s, decade-old *New Statesman*s and copies of *Vogue*. Why someone who never went outside might care to know that mustard clothes were in for autumn would forever be a mystery. The mirror on the door between the hallway and the living room was so thick with grime that nothing was visible in it.

Johnny traced a finger down it and said, 'Guess there was no need to cover this one.' Sasha scooped off a film of dust with one hand and shot him a revolted look.

'I'll be in the kitchen. She promised me the gold filigree tea glasses since I was a little girl.'

'Make sure you rinse them thoroughly.'

I made my way upstairs with the empty bag I'd brought, treading gingerly on the peeling carpet. Despite all precautions, I was nearly felled at the last moment by a small onyx tortoise that had wedged itself under one of the stair runners.

Ruth's bed still bore the depression of her body, though for the last months of her life she had slept downstairs on a divan, instructing my aunt Esther to move selected items of her hoard up and downstairs as she needed them. All attempts at preliminary tidying were met with accusations of wishing her in an early grave. I'd come in search of vintage gloves and scarves, but then I spotted her small, Queen Anne side table, looking naked without its usual load of cups and bottles. Thick rings of fluff and gunk marked the outlines of these vanished objects. They must have been filled with unusually revolting things for anyone to have bothered moving them.

I eased the table away from the wall to take a better look at it – some of the furniture was so weevilly that I remembered it frequently collapsing of its own accord, generating avalanches of rubbish and yowls from Ruth's semi-feral cats as they dodged falling ashtrays and first editions of Zeldin. She'd had at least five books on the go at any time in four languages and wouldn't answer the door without her powder on. I'd wanted to be just like her, never alone because I was surrounded by music and literature. But the Ruth who'd played Mendelssohn on the piano, and thrilled us with ghost stories about men losing control after being possessed by angry dybbuks, had grown hard to separate in my memory from the woman who'd bitten someone for attempting to bathe her and stuffed me with fig biscuits while berating me for being chubby.

'Look at you, getting older and still no boyfriend. Surely someone must want you? It's a shame none of you turned out natural blondes like me.'

Behind the table was a patch of wall that had been gouged out and then covered up with masking tape. Somebody had begun to plaster it over again but had evidently grown bored and given up. I squatted down and started to saw through the stiffened tape with my keys. It would probably be a botched wiring job, but Ruth was just as capable of having hidden a stack of Swiss francs behind the wall and it seemed best not to leave these for the movers to discover. As I pulled away the strips, I saw that the space was full of scrunched-up newspapers, tightly packed and stinking of damp. Peeking out from this second grey wall of detritus was the corner of a wooden box. It had been thrust as far back into the house as it would go, but my fingers found a purchase on one carved edge and I yanked it free, losing my balance as I did so. As I toppled backwards, the box fell open with a little puff of dust. Inside, there was nothing but a few dried rose petals, a cheap-looking metal ring and an old photograph of a smiling young woman with a dark coiffured bob, wearing a stripy shirt and loose woollen jacket, sitting on a bed in a cramped garret.

'Miri? Miri, are you seriously sleeping up here? It's filthy. Wake up, we want to leave now.'

Sasha was standing over me as I lay spreadeagled on the itchy carpet, blinking at the sunset I could see descending over the slate roofs of East Finchley. My neck hurt from the strange angle I had slept on it.

'Don't forget this. I hope you got a good haul.'

I rose unsteadily to my feet and Sasha handed me my bag. She said, 'I always thought her clothes were awful, but no doubt you'll make something quirky out of them.'

My head was heavy and my tongue sat in my mouth like a dead slug. My hair felt full of dust. I was used to being tired all the time, but passing out like this was just embarrassing.

I asked, 'Did you find anything?'

She crooked the corner of her mouth into a grin. She had always been the most beautiful of us and she knew it. Wherever we went, someone would pop up who remembered her and wanted to offer favours unasked for and undreamt of. Free meals, tickets to sold-out events, legal advice, two months in a Sicilian villa, once a bulldog puppy.

'Can you keep a secret?'

I waited, promising nothing. She opened her jacket and I saw that the inside pocket was stuffed with rolled-up paper tubes.

'Don't tell Johnny, but I found some woodblock prints I think might be the real deal. He'll just want to sell them, but they're our heirlooms.'

I nodded, wondering if her game plan was really to take them off the wall every time he came to visit. Downstairs, Johnny had laid claim to a tapestry-covered footstool. He insisted on recruiting Sasha to lug it out of the house and handed me the keys to lock up behind them. I bolted the door to the living room and walked back along the hall in the dim light, picking my way over the ladders and the flurries of unopened post. I reached for the handle of the open front door, then changed my mind and turned back to face the mirror instead. I thought I saw Sasha standing close behind me, watching as I brushed the dust from my dishevelled hair. But when I walked out onto the street, there she was smoking over by the car and providing a running commentary on

Johnny's attempts at collapsing the seats to accommodate the stool.

We crawled back through the eastbound traffic, past Polish shops, Hindu temples, and the shuttered Muddler Bar where I'd first met Lucy, who had been arguing in the smoking area with a girl with padlocks through both ears about the right way to implement anarchism.

Perhaps I had been wrong to exclude her. She couldn't see her own family any more, for reasons of safety, and I'd have liked to make her part of mine. Johnny and Sasha had been thrilled I was finally dating again in my own haphazard fashion, and immediately asked to meet her. But the idea of subjecting Lucy to my parents' obvious distaste rendered that plan impossible.

After forty-five minutes of having my knees against my cheekbones and Sasha's elbow in my ear, I needed to unwind. Thankfully, Johnny suggested a swift one, mainly so he could show us pictures of him snorkelling in the Philippines, interspersed with the grinning children whose cleft palates he had helped to sew up. He did a good impression of remembering them all by name.

'So what did everybody get for their haul?' Johnny definitely knew Sasha was up to something.

I pulled out my trophy. 'Look what I found hidden in the wall, there wasn't much inside but it's quite pretty.'

Sasha put her hand over the lid and said, 'I can't remember where I heard about this, but you should probably put that back.'

'Why, are you going to come back and take it later?' Johnny asked.

Sasha pushed the box back across the table towards me. 'I have all the memories of Ruth I need.'

To defuse matters, I proposed a toast to Ruth, difficult as she could be. The night became fragmentary after that. We asked ourselves why we didn't do this more often. Sasha peeled off home, pleading a run the next day. It was last orders and my debit card was declined, so I switched to credit and bought one for the old gent who'd been hinting he knew somewhere that stayed open later. An underground bar with no sign and a black-and-white tiled floor. A beautiful woman and her ugly, insistent husband. A different woman, in a cab, and my keys jabbing everywhere but in the lock. I could barely keep my eyes open, but she seemed impressed as my hands moved of their own volition to please her. I didn't usually have the strength to lift someone and keep them supported. Halfway through, I met the stare of my reflection in the bedroom mirror, and felt sure it was still watching us as I turned away.

I woke in chaos, mercifully alone. There was an unfamiliar pair of lacy pants beside me and a cigarette hole burnt into the centre of my pillow. I smelt stale smoke but the butt was nowhere to be seen. Through the open door I could make out a pint glass smashed on the kitchen floor and streaks of dried mud encrusted on the rug. Somehow I had managed to hang on to the bag, but not my phone. I suspected I might have looked at its empty screen one last time, devoid of messages from Lucy, and thrown it into a canal.

After some feeble efforts to clear up the evidence of the night before, I looked inside the bag and found the box, swaddled in four mock-Hermès scarves. I opened it again. There was no writing on the back of the photograph except the lone initial 'D'. My father professed a very hazy knowledge of Ruth's life at the best of times, so I couldn't ask him who the woman was. When Sasha had proposed to interview her on tape for a project at school, Ruth's response had been that she was not living history, just alive and she had no interest in raking up the past. I wrapped the box up again and put it under my bed, where it would not be taken for an ashtray or a convenient resource for one my flatmate Rodrigo's decoupage projects.

Over the next few weeks, as winter tussled back and forth with spring, I had many more nights like that one.

130

For a long time, I had been retreating further and further inside myself, tongue wordlessly numb and brain muzzy with despair. Every day my arms were heavy and my chest hollowed out. I was never warm and only grudgingly hungry. Work emails from the galleries and estates I had to haggle with over usage fees for catalogues went unanswered. I had been dragging myself through the world like an afterthought, waiting to be as dead as I felt. The growing distance between me and Lucy had been almost a comfort. If she never inquired too deeply into how I was, I'd never have to tell her that I wasn't there.

But now I laughed at sleep and when I slept, I dreamt of windy lamplit corners. *A little bar, hidden behind the door in a restaurant, that smelt of onions and cigars, where butches danced in three-piece suits and femmes shrugged off their ratty furs to join them at dodging low tables in the crowded cellar. The taste of brandy and the chalky powder collecting in the hollows of a blonde woman's neck as she ran her fingers through my bob. The same woman, spread out naked in a freezing attic room, and my hands on her, though these were not my hands.*

Awake, I brimmed over with anger and vigour and lust. I felt the tight muscles of my thighs piston as I ran for trains to private views across London and revelled in my strength. My spine straightened out to stand tall. I met the gaze of interested women, then smirked at their boyfriends, almost mouthing the words *I can outdrink you, outfuck you and most likely beat you in a fight as well*. I swiped the bad free wine from first-night openings, not even pretending to care about the artists. I walked like I was ready to swing a bottle in the world's face at the slightest provocation. My limbs moved before I could think to move them and reached out with no forethought. I received replies to emails I didn't even know I'd written, beating down the price of image permissions, telling me I'd won. The only thing that quieted my rage was booze but then I just got bolder, waking up in strange bathrooms, on strangers' sofas or in strangers' beds, walletless, with a perfect ring of bitemarks on my forearm, with business cards and scribbled numbers and, once, curled on a bare floor around a traffic cone. I drank until the liquid in my glass might as well have been water for all the difference it would make and then I kept on going. And yet in all that time I never came to real harm. Something watched me as I was nodding out, and it was thrilled at the mess I made.

Over the next few months I dragged Johnny out to bars and pubs under the guise of quality time now that he was back in London, preparing for the exams he did in between holidays spent saving the wretched of the earth.

'I just got done with work and I need a drink. Just come for a couple, I'm only down the road.'

'OK fine, a couple but no more, I have a lot to do in the morning.' And we'd meet on the corner, him in a cable-knit jumper looking impossibly fresh-faced and me in my navy coat with the ripped lining bulging out of the sleeves because I wasn't getting enough new work in to justify fixing it. Two minor galleries in Vienna had complained to a publisher that I was the rudest person they'd ever been in correspondence with, but I couldn't find the thread to read over it.

And the hands of the clock would creep around and he would start telling me about the worst things he had ever seen on the job, the woman with maggoty labia and the man who put out his own eye with a pencil and how the smell of formaldehyde made you hungry, then guilty for feeling hungry. The children half crushed under buildings during earthquakes, who he could do nothing to help because morphine was always rationed. How he filled out cremation certificates for extra cash and sat being screamed at by bereaved families for not performing miracles. It was never just a couple.

The dreams kept coming, no matter whether I drifted off or passed out after hours of Red Bull mixers and powders off the backs of strangers' hands. *The blonde woman under me gasping and reaching out a cold hand to grip the small of my*

back. Frying two eggs in a blackened pan on a tiny stove, then walking together down long, tree-lined avenues, gloved fingers not quite touching. The first bright yellow crocuses. My woollen jacket, hanging on the only chair, still rimed with frost. Two sets of papers bearing unfamiliar names. Stuffing my best clothes into an old leather suitcase and shouting at her that we needed to leave, then giving up when she didn't even get up from the bed.

As spring progressed into summer, Johnny grew unresponsive. His latest set of exams were not for months, but he claimed he had to stay in and revise or pick up locum shifts. I finally managed to lure him out for ramen one afternoon.

'Why are you being so boring? We haven't lived in the same place at the same time in years.'

'I need a rest. The house is a state and I've been wearing the same jeans for a week. Don't you think you could do with a night in too?'

I had a batch of invoices I needed to send out to clients, but then again . . . I watched a tall woman in a dark grey coat as she strolled out of the restaurant, slowly pulling on her gloves. I was fairly certain she had just been giving me the eye.

I asked him, 'Do you think it's possible to inherit memories, if they're strong enough?'

'Depends what you mean by memories. There's a lot of evidence that if you put rats under enough stress, several generations of their progeny will have elevated cortisol levels.'

'OK Doctor Rosenthal, but I'm not talking about rats. I ... I ...' my windpipe clamped shut, and as I started coughing, I felt my lips seal, as if someone had pulled tight an invisible zipper.

Johnny's eyes scanned up and down, I saw him taking in my left boot beginning to gape at the toe, my yellow-stained fingers and the little web of broken veins haloing both my nostrils. He assumed what must have been his bedside manner and softly placed his hand on my arm. I could feel how dry his palms were from antibacterial gel.

'How are things with Lucy? Are you still together?'

He looked at me and tilted his head slightly to the side, in the manner of one who has learnt to expect confessions if he applies enough patient silence.

The seal broke. 'Why do you want to know?'

'She isn't making you very happy, is she?'

'She's happy enough. We have our own lives.'

'Does she know about ...?' He'd seen me sneak off to toilets and alleyways with women we'd met on nights out, but perhaps he'd been too afraid to ask outright if I was cheating.

'It's allowed. I'm sure she's doing much the same. At least, she's busy with something, otherwise maybe she'd answer her bloody phone.'

Lucy and I had enjoyed a perfectly cordial dinner together two weeks before, which began with her

135

apologising for not having enough time to see me and finished with her remarking that she was thinking of learning Chinese to seduce one of her colleagues. Then she stuck me with the bill. I had only had the dumplings.

He asked, 'Did you ever meet Ruth's friend Joan? She lived with Ruth for a while when we were young.'

I scanned my memory, pitted as it was with darkness and uncertainty. 'I don't think I ever did. What are you getting at?'

'Apparently she moved out because of Ruth's hoarding, but Mum told me she still asked to come sit shiva. Your father had a fit and wouldn't let her.'

The existence of Joan was news to me, though my father's reaction to it was not wholly surprising, given his determined incuriosity around the topic of my own 'friends'. I envied Ruth's having attracted someone devoted enough to mourn her even after enduring clumps of matted hair trailing round the stair runners, multiple booklets of expired margarine coupons and the death-watch beetle colony. I resolved to drink on the matter and held out my sake bowl for a refill.

Johnny poured out one final glug from the carafe and cleared his throat. 'That house was a disgrace but Ruth wasn't the only person in our family with problems. I know it's not an easy subject, but it's pretty striking how many of us aren't quite all there.'

'Look, I love your mum, but she *really* enjoyed the seventies. It's not surprising she's mental now, it sounds like she spent half that decade taking LSD in squats round Notting Hill.'

'That's really unfair. She's just a bit of a hippie still. Anyway, when I said problems I didn't mean her.'

'The primal screaming therapy? The astral travel? The time she convinced herself she could see auras and said that mine was mauve streaked with lime green?'

'OK, the aura phase was a lot. And I had to fake her signature to get my BCG. I was talking about Naomi though – we all know what she was like before she did a one-eighty and married that Modern Orthodox guy, the holiday to Bali she went on a few years ago was actually rehab. And the less said about the South African Rosenthals, the better.'

'For god's sake, Johnny, you've made your point, we're all nuts. Now are you going to get us another sake?'

He caught the waiter's eye and pointed at the empty carafe.

'You're not hearing me. Something obviously runs in the family even if nobody likes to talk about it. Maybe you should look after yourself a bit better?'

I paused to drain my cup then snapped, 'And what about you, Johnny? Or are you the exception to the rule?' I went on in what I thought was a credible imitation of my mother's voice: 'Remember to tell Grandma about your essay, Miri, you know Johnny gets all A★s without even trying. Johnny's girlfriend is coming on holiday with us this year, Miri, make sure you're nice to her, I think she might be a Montefiore. The very brightest and *sanest* of us all.'

The waiter plunked the steaming earthenware bottle down onto the table. Suddenly Johnny looked very tired. He sighed. 'Just don't say I didn't try.'

The following night, I resentfully took Johnny's advice and stayed in. I didn't want to go to the cinema alone. Lucy had sounded frustrated the last time I called.

'I can't be everything to you. Instead of waiting for me to be freer, why don't you go see your school friends?'

'They're all getting engaged and buying houses. The last time I went to a party someone said the phrase "I wouldn't get out of bed and piss for less than £50k".'

'Straight people.'

Unspoken between us were the stories I'd told her about my attempts to join LGBTsoc during university. At the Christmas drinks, the vice president, whom I'd never met before, had said, 'So I hear you're Jewish. Are your whole family Zionists, then?' I'd gone on to have a variety of discouraging interactions with well-intentioned people from the home counties who hid their discomfort with me behind my imagined discomfort with Muslims. After all, what could I possibly have in common with people whose holidays were ignored, whose customs were ridiculed and who were presumed always to be members of a nefarious fifth column? If I was going into queer spaces, I had to be a good half

bottle of wine deep already and then keep hold of myself
so I wouldn't start talking back.

I laid out my softest fluffy socks and made a big mug
of rooibos to drink in the bath. Dribbled lavender oil
into the tiny, greying tub and watched it opalesce on the
surface, streaking my fingers through the warm water to
change the patterns in the gleaming spill. The scented
steam crept down my nostrils and throat, gently burning
smoke-crusted lungs and making everything feel clean
again. I shrugged off my clothes. The vertebrae of my
spine were creaky and my hips clicked when I bent. I
leant over the sink, poring over the accumulated damage in the mirror. My hand darted out to grab a kohl
pencil which was sitting in the glass by the tap. I tried to
return it to the glass, but my hand snapped back like a
rubber band, just missing my eye. I dropped the pencil on
the floor and watched it roll away under a cabinet, then
turned back to stare down my reflection. The pencil had
left a black mark, from which a tear of red was beginning
to form. Not trusting my right hand, I reached over with
my left to try and rub it away. I did not break the mirror's gaze. She blinked, slowly, almost lasciviously. I froze.
Tried to do the scanning exercise I'd been taught to cure
insomnia, clenching and unclenching every muscle from
my toes up to my jaw. The mirror slowly fogged over
with the steam from the bath, I wiped my hand across

to clear a space and watched intently but the reflection didn't move again. Eventually, I turned away to get in the bath. Both legs gave out with a slam against the floor. On my knees, stomach shoved against the outside of the tub, my face plunged into the water. Not quite a hand, but an insistent pressure at the back of my neck, no matter how I bucked and pushed with scrabbling fingers at the slick bottom of the tub. I thrashed and gurgled and forced my head above the water a few times, eyes burning from the oil, but soon everything went dark.

I came up for air in short, confusing bursts. Standing naked in my room, winding an old scarf tight around my chest. Scrabbling to find the foul plum brandy kept hidden for true emergencies. Clinging to the orange pole inside a train, pretending not to hear a group of boys laughing at me. Nothing else until I felt cold metal and saw black ink drying on my wrist. Darkness again. Strobe lights. *O bella ciao, bella ciao* the music pumped and thrilled and deafened as the speakers battered me with soundwaves. The damp air was rich with sweat, the girl at my waist dipped low and then ground back onto me, grinning over her bare shoulder, the rivets of her jeans catching just right. I grabbed her waist and spun her round to face me, kissing her neck while stealthily looking past her. This was definitely the Muddler, I recognised those neon cartoon murals. The oily bitterness of cheap tonic coated my tongue. The girl pulled away for a moment to sweep back her long dark hair, it caught the light like polished lacquer. I was boiling hot, dressed bafflingly in old black cords and a calico men's shirt I'd picked up years ago and never worn. The pace of the electronic drumbeats rose, building to a peak and she was leaning in to kiss me *bella ciao, ciao, ciao* I was out again before the drop.

The blonde woman, with a dull silver ring on her finger, sitting a few tables away in a crowded cafe, carefully not looking at me. She had taken my advice, but wasn't taking me with her. A solitary egg burning on the stove. Crocuses wilting in a mug. The smoky bar again, half empty, and the sound of breaking glass upstairs. A crowded train, stinking of shit and panic. A black, inverted triangle imposed over a yellow one.

The next morning, after I had prised myself away from the salt-sweat back of my stranger and off her single mattress on the floor, I staggered onto the Northern line and somehow made it to the coffee shop Sasha and I had promised to meet in, only twenty minutes late. The shop couldn't make its mind up whether it was a deli, a lifestyle boutique or a cafe. I decided to pony up £8 I didn't have for a cardboard box of unidentifiable grains and bits of roasted parsnip. Both of us had silently noted

141

the bacon-and-egg-stuffed bagels sitting by the counter with raised brows.

She told me about her new boyfriend Simon, a barrister who liked to run triathlons and foster kittens in his spare time. I was having trouble distinguishing him from Sam, the pentathlon-running solicitor ex-boyfriend. Sasha rapped perfect, nude-coloured oval gel nails against the table tiles, her double espresso long drained to its dregs. The lip balm sat open on the table, as it had since I'd arrived.

'. . . And you should see his flat, it's got exposed brick walls and granite counters and a view out over the river. He said the other night that he'd always hoped to propose to someone with that view . . . though it's far too soon to think of that, of course! The prints look so good there. You must come over soon and meet him. We could have a double date – are you still seeing Lucy?'

'Seeing would be putting it a bit strongly.' I speared another lump of parsnip.

'Oh. I'm sorry to hear that. Well come anyway and meet the kittens.' She reached into her soft teal leather bag, a single golden bee printed in fine lines on the flap.

Just as I was preparing to ask her for the multitude of kitten pictures she clearly wanted to show me, my dying phone buzzed with a text from Rodrigo.

Hey hope you're well :) I respect whatever lesbian witch-craft you're doing but please can you keep it to your own room? Really freaked out my date last night. Thanks! x
PS we're out of kitchen roll

Swiftly after that, I received a photo of the bathroom mirror. Rodrigo stood in a cream polo shirt in the background. He held the remnants of my broken china mug from one curled finger. On the glass the words

VERGISS MEINEN NAMEN NICHT

were written in reddish, flaky-looking letters.

'Whose name are you supposed to remember?' Seeing my horrified face, Sasha had peered over to look. She paused, reading the text as well, then said, 'I didn't realise Ruth's death upset you so much. I'm sorry for what I said about you guys never being there, I know you found it really hard to see her like that.'

I was about to deny everything but realised just in time how bad that sounded. My head was full of jumbled thoughts and non-explanations. Eventually, I said, 'I wish she'd been open about her life, but I know she wasn't able to.'

'I miss her too. There's so much no one will tell us.'

When I made it home, I reached under my bed and unwrapped the wooden box, running my fingertips over its dents and tracing the blond whorls in the grain. The hinges had little golden curlicues shaped like leaves. As I tipped the box forward to look closer, I expected to hear a little thud as the ring hit the inner lip of the frontmost edge, but when I opened it, there was nothing but a thin layer of ash inside.

Lucy came over and I roasted a whole chicken. After we'd eaten she lay sprawled on the sofa as I stripped the carcass. I saw her look at me with a grimace as I carefully poured the fat into a jug to make kneidlach with. Getting all her sculptures ready for the winter showcase at uni had stressed her out so much she'd stopped speaking to me for a month, but now she'd finally received her mark. I was just pleased to be making a fuss of her again. I would walk a mile before taking the stone out of my shoe, but regularly fantasised about wrapping her in blankets and feeding her soup, somewhere quiet away from the rest of the world.

We lay entwined on the sofa, listening to *Fingal's Cave* while the candles burnt low in their bottles. Lucy had her phone out and was scrolling through her timeline as I looked over her shoulder. She hated being asked to put it away.

She said, 'I'm so sick of seeing everyone's posts about how they're leaving England, it's such a privileged response to the problem. Some of us are stuck here.'

'Not everyone who moves country is rich, people leave their homes with nothing if they have to.'

'I just think it's selfish to get up and go every time something is wrong instead of trying to fix things.' She shifted to lay her head in the hollow between my collarbones.

'Sometimes problems are too big to fix.'

Lucy sat up and snapped, 'How would you know what a big problem looks like? Nothing's going to affect you, anyway.'

I stood up before I knew I was moving. It was happening again. Lucy yipped and fought to stop herself overbalancing. My arm shot out and my hand opened to grasp her jacket from where she'd flung it over a chair. I tried to unclench but it was stuck fast. Tendrils of rage fluttered in my stomach and pushed up, I felt them probing and coiling round my throat. My mouth opened, lips contorted into a rigid hiss.

'Get . . . the . . . fuck . . . out.'

'Oh my god, Miri, you're ridiculous. I'm having such a hard time right now and you just overreact to everything, we talked about this.'

My other hand grabbed her satchel and slung it gaping open over one shoulder, then stuffed one of the bags of chicken morsels from the counter inside it. My legs stayed stiff like a tin soldier's, marching me over to the door to fling it open.

She looked at me coldly, rising to her feet. I tried to say sorry, to say anything else at all but my lips wouldn't open. All the features of her face I loved the most seemed magnified in the candlelight.

'I know you aren't trying to manipulate me, but when you get so upset like this it makes me feel manipulated.'

145

I felt a tear bud and swell in one eye and prayed for it to break, but it didn't fall.

'. . . Get . . . out.'

My hands threw her jacket and satchel out into the hall and when she went to retrieve them, slammed the door and bolted it. I heard her gather herself and stomp out, muttering 'crazy bitch' under her breath.

It was Uncle Marcus's turn to host and I was running late. The smell of cumin and garlic drifted down the freezing cold passageway outside his house and I followed it, nose in the air, nearly tripping over the three big crates of wine and beer sat just outside the door.

The drone of conversation rose and fell while the bell kept chiming. Eventually Cousin Naomi opened the door, somehow even more hugely pregnant, one hand kneading absent-mindedly against her back.

'Come in, come in, your mum and dad have been here for an hour already. Are you on your own?' Her emerald wrap dress ballooned into big romantic sleeves and fell in a swoop of abstracted florals to hit her leg at mid-calf. I could never tell if she was donning chic modest-wear or just determined to cover the scars on her arms.

'Well they're here, so what do you think?' Then quickly, so I didn't have to deal with her pitying me, I asked 'How's Boaz?'

'Oh he's wonderful, as ever. He just got made a partner.'

Boaz had insisted on my aunt and uncle ransacking the entire house to track down their ketubah before he would set a date with Naomi. His adherence to tradition had not made him a family favourite.

After I had given seven or eight different people the same heavily edited information about how well I was doing as a freelancer and Aaron had interrogated me about whether I'd filed my taxes this year, Marcus made us all sit down for dinner. He and Esther had met on a kibbutz in the early eighties, then promptly left when the longer-term members started training them how to use guns and they'd realised the true cost of staying. One of the happier legacies of that time was that Marcus had become a fantastic cook. The long table was dotted with platters of grilled courgettes and bowls of steaming rice studded with spiced lentils and crispy onions.

Johnny and I were squished onto two halves of a splintery wooden bench when I heard Naomi say to Sasha in a low voice, 'Don't tell Boaz I asked you, but . . . let's say we were to have a girl . . . I'd been thinking of Ruth, but then I remembered it's his aunt's name, so we can't. Do you know if there're any other old family names we could use?'

The tendrils twitched and wrapped around my throat even tighter, squeezing with a rhythmic pulse, like something too big for my jaw was working its way out. I bent over and wheezed into a napkin, choking like I was about to be sick, though nothing seemed to come out, or at least, nothing English. *Vergiss . . . nicht.* I shook and thumped my chest, ignoring two proffered glasses of water. 'D—, D—, D—' Finally I managed to draw breath. I found words lingering in my mouth as if they had been burnt into my tongue. 'Call her Deborah.'

Naomi's face twisted with pain for a moment, then she put a hand to her belly and smiled.

No Dominion

... Darkness and silence and cold. Startled, then languorous again. Cold blackness covered me. I blinked into the black, surprised to have eyelids. I lay in the silt like it was my mattress, looked up so far I saw nothing but light. I looked away, then looked back. The light was a pinkish colour and confined mostly within a small margin far above. Enough was beginning to filter down that I started to perceive what lay round me. Small bushes of coral surrounded a greater structure, bright reds and muted blues, with fish darting in between branches. I made my way over to the nearest outgrowth, looked closely with eyes suddenly hungry for colour and detail. It seemed to be growing on a kind of plinth. I bent down, saw an edge to the plinth and along that edge a suitcase catch. In among the rosette-like growths, I thought I could make out a man's razor, and not far from that some small scissors. Shapes too straight to find in nature. I went from clump to clump, observed a hairbrush and a shoe. There was a book, splayed open and so petrified I could not read it.

I began to feel afraid.

The body of the reef seemed to have grown in a rough X-shape, though one axis was much fatter than the other. The reef was humpbacked in the middle. I didn't want to peer down through the rupture at the highest point, to have

149

my fear confirmed. I climbed up on it using the rounder growths to grip, feet sliding in the mucus, the rosettes' ridges felt bigger underfoot. I could not see very far inside, just a few rows of seats and an encrusted trolley. The octopus in the aisle seemed startled. Where were the others?

As if responding to a call, low-lying forms beneath the sand began to stir. A man sat up and rubbed his brow. As I backed away from the ruins of the plane, I trod upon a blackened skull. The flesh was rapidly pasting itself together, like a papier-mâché sculpture of a face I'd known. Two separate shapes moved through the sand and united, legs and torso. A partially preserved hand skittered across the ocean floor to find its wrist. My own flesh looked strangely pearlescent, poreless as a mannequin. I stood and watched them rising like an army with the dawn; they shook themselves out and waited. When all of us had been assembled, men and women, our agelessness was more apparent. I felt a sudden tug, as if a hook had been guided through some internal eye. This now pulled me inexorably upwards. We all went together, legs kicking, open mouths dumb. Up through unknown fathoms till the reef below looked like a spiny pebble. The air felt thin when we broke the surface and kept on hurtling skywards, jerking like marionettes. The air froze my skin as I shot into the dense, wet white clouds, waves shrinking from sight beneath us. I panicked as the undercarriage of the plane drew closer, a great grey whirring, screeching steel expanse through which we passed with an audible pop back into the sticky pleather arms of our assigned seats.

You were my consolation every time I travelled, though I never told you. My neighbour read her book quietly, as the man by the window clambered past us clutching a razor to freshen up in the bathroom, while I sat and thought of you. As the flight attendants ran through their dumbshow, the screeching of the air along the plane increased but they went on with their routine unmoved. They had done this all so often and I had sat through it so many times I knew their moves by heart. I wondered if I should tell you, if you'd care. I always concluded that you would care, so I shouldn't. Took out my memories and touched them gently like icons, gold leaf beginning to peel at the places most caressed. Despite my fear, this was the time that I liked most, in that grey twilight between the arbitrary demarcations of hours, days and minutes. In transit, there was time no longer, our routines were always the same. Here, I could not count how long I'd wasted living for you, living in you. I held my seat arms impotently long after the plane righted itself, searching the attendants' faces for dismay. Their haggard good cheer rendered them identical, would I know if I had seen them all before? We had got more than halfway before we began losing height. First slowly, then faster and faster when nothing could be done to stop the falling. I gave too much to the thought of you, but you would be something to hold in my mind at the last. I held onto you even as we hit the water

into the darkness and silence and cold . . .

Stay A While

I.

'It's not an orgy without five people, minimum. Everyone knows that.' Livia watched Roland crushing the cube of brown sugar into his espresso with the back of a teaspoon, absorbing her pronouncement. Every time she visited his basement flat, there seemed to be another horse painting. The bachelor uncle who had left this place to him had been a proud member of the household cavalry. Livia's mother remained comically desperate for her to marry Roland, but then again she had never seen the whorls of black fungus on his bathroom ceiling.

He said, 'I thought you said we should avoid having an orgy because it would precipitate the destruction of our friendship group.'

Livia poked a finger into the molten pool forming in one of the pillar candles Roland habitually lit against the gloom, then withdrew when it went numb, wax hardening around the digit. She wanted so badly to feel alive again.

'I did say that once ... but if there are fewer people at a Black Mass than at an orgy, that's not very pleasing to Satan, is it? You were moaning only the other day about how bored you are, and it's not like you believe in the soul any more, so selling it should hardly matter.'

He sniffed the coffee and put it down. The horse Livia could see over his shoulder had a manic expression, like it was considering biting someone in uniform.

Roland finally relented. 'I'll ask Bonnie, but I don't think she'll be keen. She was confirmed, you know, she takes that sort of thing quite seriously.'

'All the better – James was an altar boy, having two proper Catholics makes it much more blasphemous. Let's take some control over our lives, rather than just letting them drift past.'

In the end there were six of them: James's wife Yu-Jin was always pleased by novelty, and Alexa, as a former goth, told Livia she simply had to be there.

Roland had come to collect them from the station in a Peugeot so old they'd had to drive with all the windows down in lieu of air-conditioning. Gazing out of the window at the Wiltshire hills, Livia shifted in her seat to support the pleasant weight of Alexa's sandaled feet resting on her bare thighs. A large, dark bee drifted into the car for a moment and then flew out. Soon they were chuntering up the drive towards Rakeswood, with two ornamental lakes on either side of them. The left-hand lake had swans paddling rather listlessly across its surface, while the right was empty. An ancestor of Roland's had built the house in the late eighteenth century after finding success as a planter in Jamaica, a detail Roland would not admit to unless asked directly. A vast cedar tree spread its boughs over the lawn, the branches almost touching the walls at their furthest extent. Some of these branches

were so long and so old that they had to be supported by wooden crutches, something Livia had otherwise
only seen in Vietnamese mausolea. She fell into a reverie
of what the evening ahead might contain – perhaps it
would alleviate the boredom that grew ever harder to
shrug off with each new and outlandish experience she
tried in her other life away from them.

'Why didn't you tell me Roland lived in a mansion?'
Alexa asked, lighting a cigarette.

No comment came from the driver's seat.

Livia said, 'Oh sorry, I thought it was sort of implicit.
Do you not remember that picture of Roland and his
dog in front of the ha-ha?'

'The what?'

'It's a kind of fancy ditch. Anyway, you'd only do that if
it were too tacky to take a picture in front of your actual
house.'

Alexa gave a choking little laugh, and Roland pulled
the car into its spot just round the side of the house.
Bonnie had been leaning against a column, waiting for
them. She came over to the car and took the cigarette
right out of Alexa's hand, getting in two drags before
Alexa made it out of the car door. Livia lugged her suitcase into the hall, past the cases of taxidermy puffins and
four generations' worth of walking sticks, and dragged it
up the spiral staircase to her room.

Apparently, Roland's father was on a convenient fish-
ing trip in Germany and the housekeeper had been sent
back early to Little Raking. Due to her absence, Roland

was making liberal use of the hotplate, which Livia felt it necessary to keep a watchful eye on, so the veal didn't get tough. Some of this group had yet to be entirely won over to debauchery and she'd determined that everything had to be just so. Why should she continue to keep her two lives separate, when she could have company in Hell?

They caught each other up on the various triumphs and failures of the week. Yu-jin was trying unsuccessfully to wiggle out of going back to Kiev to be maid of honour for a childhood friend's wedding. Bonnie was in the middle of casting her new production of *Peer Gynt* and so had to contend with unreliable actors, unrealistic demands by the venue and uncertainty over why she was putting herself through this yet again. Livia had been banned from cast parties on the basis that she couldn't stop sleeping with Bonnie's actors.

Alexa had been busying herself with the seduction of her new boyfriend's best friend's girlfriend. Her boyfriend had given her his approval, but it was as yet unclear how much the best friend knew or was prepared to know. Livia entertained herself by speculating on the degree to which the girlfriend must resemble her (and the girl before her, and the girl before that).

Although it was Roland's house, James was to be Master of Ceremonies. After Livia, he seemed the least contented with his good fortune and what his natural gifts might bring. James had once told her he envied animals their freedom from the responsibility of choice. He sat turning his wineglass, watching how high the legs reached up the bowl.

'It seems a shame to have gone to all this trouble and still not be able to procure ourselves a virgin. I know Livia is serving as altar, but, no offence intended, she's been depucelated for over a decade.'

Livia's hair was sticking to her face with the June humidity – and her growing anticipation. James could always be relied upon to escalate matters. She attempted to sweep it back in one motion and, having failed, replied, 'It is a shame, but short of heading into Little Raking and requesting to borrow one of Roland's tenants' daughters, I think we may just have to make do.'

Roland had finally rescued the veal from the hotplate and was holding the dish while Yu-jin helped herself. 'Oh yes, I can imagine that going over well. Good evening, Mr Moore, I trust your fence hasn't been giving you any trouble. We just need Sophie for a couple of hours, and we promise we'll return her mostly intact.'

Yu-jin passed on the dish with shaky arms and said, 'I am not getting back in the car with you, James, you've been drinking since lunchtime.'

Alexa asked, 'Surely at least one of the boys must be a virgin in the arse?'

James scoffed and drained his wineglass.

Bonnie said, 'I'm pretty sure you've still got that virginity, don't you?'

Roland, in a sudden hurry to dispense refills, reached all the way across the table for the decanter, speckling the tablecloth with rosy droplets.

Livia swallowed a mouthful of veal. It had survived its wait reasonably well. 'But you boarded for seven years, what's wrong with you?'

'I told you, I was very Christian. I could barely masturbate without feeling guilty,' said Roland.

'Are you sure we can't tempt you to join in, Bonnie? Just think of it as a piece of immersive theatre. It's a harmless bit of fun and you might get some new ideas to play with,' said Livia.

'Unlike you, I know the difference between art and life.'

'That's a failure of imagination.'

After dinner had concluded, Bonnie went off upstairs to write grant applications and James set to work on a batch of French 75s, dropping a pink pill into each one as a garnish. He and Alexa then slunk off to prepare, leaving them to wait in the drawing room though it was still light outside. The room was large and filled with Meissen shepherdesses, Victorian hair art in glass-fronted cabinets and dark wood netsuke of copulating deer. Roland was playing with an engraved fan case, slapping the palm of his hand with it every time he made a point about the pointlessness of jealousy. Yu-jin sat in an armchair bouncing her knee up and down and smoking with gusto. Livia watched as the cogs and levers under the glass hood of the clock on the mantelpiece guided them ever closer to midnight.

II.

Livia had recently received a phone call from her first serious girlfriend during which Annie apologised for raping her. She had been very drunk and upset on the phone, and when Livia told her it was OK, it turned out the call was a precursor to inviting Livia over to sleep with her again. It took Livia a while to get her off the line, and before this had been achieved, she'd told Livia she was still in love with her. She was drunk enough that this seemed sincere, rather than an attempt at cack-handed manipulation.

The night Annie was referring to had been a long time ago, during the final months of their relationship. Livia had never thought of it before she'd been remind-ed. They'd been in Livia's parents' country house, argu-ing in bed together with the lights out. She and Annie had agreed that she was Annie's possession and Livia wore a ribbon round her neck to signify this, but her two best friends were in the room next door and she didn't want them to hear. Annie didn't hold her down, but she had known Livia didn't want to and did it any-way. She'd known that Annie was perfectly capable of breaking up with her on the spot, so she lay there crying in the dark as Annie grew more and more frustrated that Livia's faked enjoyment was not sufficiently convincing. The most vivid part of this newly excavated memory was Livia's annoyance that her teardrops were running directly along her cheekbones and into the cups of her ears. She hated getting water in her ears.

In the phone call, Annie had given what passed between them a name, and in doing so, invited it back into her mind. Livia had been so successful at forgetting, she had not even known it was there to be forgotten. She had not been sure what to make of this recovered information, and resolved not to tell her friends. Of all the women she had loved, Annie had been the only one to love her back. She was trying hard to find this irony amusing.

III.

When the gong sounded, they re-joined James and Alexa in the folly at the far end of the lawn. A sound system had been concealed in a nearby box hedge and the air was filled with a low liturgical chanting. James had changed into a black cassock, with black rubber gloves covering his hands. He handed out black hooded robes for the other two to put on. Alexa was already naked under hers, save for a black harness strapped around her breasts in the shape of a seven-pointed star, and two great curling horns that rose from her hair. In her left hand she held a censer which gave off sickly sweet smoke. A raised marble slab lay at the centre of the folly, with tufts of moss growing from its veins. The slab had absorbed none of the day's heat, and Livia was already tensing her body as she undressed to lie upon it. The cold tickled, but she was supposed to be stiff as a board. She must not laugh; the others needed this pageantry to embark on anything halfway daring. She felt James spread her legs and place a chalice brimming with wine between them, and on top of that, she saw him lay down a folded red silk handkerchief which she guessed must contain the host she'd stolen from a church the week before.

Alexa lit two black candles from one of the many which were guttering on the steps and alcoves of the folly, then placed one in each of Livia's hands. James stood between her legs and began to recite: '*In nomine magni dei nostri Satanas, introibo ad altare Domini Inferi . . .*'

James motioned for them to be still, and then took a tiny vial of LSD from his sleeve. He poured out its contents into a silver bowl that was already filled with water and swirled them with his gloved hand, flicking droplets into the faces of the others until half the liquid was gone. Then he leant over Livia with the bowl and poured some of the mixture down her throat. It was faintly bitter and soapy tasting, though no thicker than normal water.

Standing a little way behind her head, she heard James say, '*Domine Satanas, ut placatus accipias diesque nostras in felicitate disponas.*' Livia watched from upside down, as Roland bent low before the inverted cross they'd placed at the back of an alcove, his chin flat on the alcove's edge, arms prostrated on the stone. She saw Alexa put down the censer and lift his cassock. Alexa proffered a little red enamel box of clear jelly to James, who moistened two

161

gloved forefingers in it, then held Roland's neck down with his left forearm so he wouldn't struggle. Livia was pleased to find that it was still easy for her to muster the icy, unintrusive interest she usually felt watching other people have sex. When James was done, he said 'Hail Satan' in a loud voice, and the others responded 'Amen', including Roland, who was at this point kneeling on the floor, trying to collect himself.

Sounds became deeper and the flames brighter against the darkness. Livia felt flushed with warmth, her nipples stiffening as the air moved over them. Yu-jin's face looked serene in the candlelight, stilled by total concentration. Behind Yu-jin, she could see the branches of the cedar swaying and twisting very slightly in the breeze and finally felt the delicious whisper of fear she had been waiting for. Even if she wanted to, it was too late to back out now; whatever James had made her drink was beginning to take effect.

Alexa said, 'Now that we've made an offering, we should ask for something in return.'

There was silence for a moment. The others had been so caught up in planning for the ceremony that they had not agreed upon an object for their prayers. It took Livia a significant effort to speak the words she'd planned, as if she were carrying them across a huge distance. 'Ask Him to prove that we have souls to sell.'

Without acknowledging her words, James took the red silk cloth and removed the host. '*Hoc est corpus Jesu Christi*,' he said, touching the wafer between Livia's breasts and then between her legs. Where it touched her, she felt a flash of heat, as if it might burn her skin.

Then he crushed the host in his fist and sprinkled the fine dust over her stomach, while Alexa withdrew a small pouch of cocaine and mixed the two together in a pile. Livia held her stomach taut, as Alexa raked it into lines and each member of the congregation inhaled their portion through a silver straw, washing it down with wine from the chalice, before kneeling to kiss Alexa's bared left buttock. As the altar, Livia was exempt – besides, she had done far worse with Alexa in private. Livia tried to count each person's line as it went, so she would know when to relax, but there seemed to be more lines than she'd reckoned, or else she wasn't counting properly. After James was finished with his line, he began the final prayer:

'Our Father which art in Hell, hallowed be Thy name. Thy kingdom is come, Thy will is done on Earth as it is in Hell. We take this night our rightful due ...'

Livia lost the struggle to stay lucid. She was lying under the world, in her little sarcophagus, as the seasons continued above her.

Her sarcophagus was stored beneath a vast gallery where she was simultaneously walking beside an unknown companion, through a long high-ceilinged room, filled with glass cases, and in every case her mummified body was laid out with its leather-brown face and collapsed nose, thin hair still clinging to its skull. Even though she closed her lids she could still see herself looking back with yellowed gummy eyes. Both she and it were crumbling to dust as her companion asked, 'What would you give me, to be whole?'

IV.

A month or so after these events, Livia met Belle in what was called the High Protocol room of a night she favoured in South London. She was well liked at Plinth for her willingness to put on a show. This was her world and people knew her. Her friends would not come here and she would not think to ask them. Livia sat on the floor in seiza, staring off into the middle distance. In this room, no one wearing a collar was allowed on the sofas, or to speak unless spoken to. The collar sat uneasily around her neck – no one had claimed her for their own since Annie, but it was a club rule to signal one's role. Most of the women present were only interested in submissive men, though they would periodically use her shoulders as footrests. Belle was small and dark and wearing heelless boots which made her feet resemble hooves. She wanted to know how long Livia had been waiting, but Livia said she wasn't sure. Every movement Belle made was so purposeful that Livia had to wonder if she were a former dancer, or perhaps ex-military. Belle drained her champagne flute and took up the flogger that had been resting by her side on the banquette, trailing its falls up Livia's bare arm, before whisking them away and asking if this was what she really wanted.

'Yes, of course it is.'

'You're absolutely sure?' A smile was beginning to form about Belle's lips.

'I want to.' Livia shuffled closer on her knees, numb from waiting, eager to be punished.

'Tell me again.'

Livia was getting annoyed now, but not unpleasantly so. Belle said nothing, so eventually she snapped, 'I'm not exactly new on the scene, you know. I'm old enough not to mess you about and too young to deny myself anything. I know exactly what I want.'

Belle leant in and kissed the centre of her forehead. Her lips were cool and soft.

'That's more like it. Get on your feet and come with me.'

There were two St Andrew's crosses soldered to a black metal frame in the centre of the club, and as they walked together towards these, Belle's hand resting gently on her shoulder, they passed another structure, not unlike an open-sided iron trellis. Inside that was a row of five men lying shirtless on the ground and two petite women in stilettos walking across them. The women gripped the trellis roof above them to vary the amount of pressure on the men. On the cross opposite, Livia, a beautiful queen in full pageant drag was having hot wax dripped onto her chest by a woman in a red latex cheongsam. Belle raised Livia's hands up by their heavy cuffs and clipped them to the cross one after the other, so that she was facing away from her.

165

Livia felt the rush of panic she always experienced just after giving up control. What if she had finally put herself beyond rescue? Belle started slowly, hitching up her dress to slap the backs of her legs. Occasionally she felt Belle stop and run her hands along her inner thighs, getting bolder as she became more certain Livia would let her do whatever she liked. She often broke the rhythm of her slaps, so that Livia would remain in suspense rather than being able to relax into the sensation. Every few minutes, she wondered if she could bear much more of this, and then told herself to wait it out before it started to feel pleasurable again. In these moments she was all body, no longer separated from herself.

Belle leant in and said, 'I've been enjoying your reactions, but if the pain gets too much, tell me to stop. We'll just wait and savour it together.'

She unzipped Livia's dress to lay her shoulders bare and graduated to the whip. This was the good stuff, the pain so pure and clear that it didn't hurt at all. The frozen fire, the burning ice. She would have let Belle continue until the bones poked through her skin.

At some point, Belle stopped by herself and let down Livia's hands, leading her over to a low couch by the wall. One of the house slaves, identifiable by the roses pinned to their outfits, stopped by with two glasses of water. She lay, still half undressed, with her head in Belle's lap, the cool leather of the couch tingling against her bared back, as Belle stroked her hair and told her she'd done well, and that there would be more pain next time.

V.

Livia's mother had spent a decade trying to persuade her she should spend her life getting fucked by some wealthy man she could not love, before giving up and deciding to view her as a failure. She remained uncertain whether her mother had thought that she could change Livia's desires or just hoped to break her will. Between this battle and her insistence that Livia should be thin, pretty and demure, it became clear she thought she owned her. That Livia was something which could be owned.

'How could you know what you want, you're far too young.'

'You're just saying that to be difficult, you're trying to get a reaction out of me.'

'Don't you know that everyone who loves you will leave you in the end?'

Later, she was told both that these things had never been said and that if they had been said, it was only out of concern. That she had worried her mother so much she'd had no choice but to hurt her and keep on hurting her and wasn't it time she stopped going on about all that, it had been such a long time ago and Livia had turned out fine.

Her mother did love her, Livia knew that with certainty. But in the world for which she had been intended, you were either a prodigy or a disaster. By the time she was twenty-two, Livia had known three people who had killed themselves after failing their exams. Yet more had needed to go into rehab or experienced severe break-downs. When she'd still believed in therapy, it had been impossible to go to her therapist's office without en-countering either a schoolmate or the children of family friends on her way in.

Livia's mother was a generous parent; for the most part Livia wanted the things she had been taught to want and she gave those things to her or helped her to get them. But the one thing Livia couldn't have was a gen-uine apology, because her mother still believed she had been right.

The only way to dissuade her of this would have been to show her the full extent of the damage, which Livia was afraid to do, in case this put any further privacy out of reach entirely.

And yet she had more freedom than most women who had ever lived.

VI.

The basement at ArteMs was heaving with girls in mesh tops, with blue-powdered brows and shaven heads. Gold lycra, tight polka-dot dresses and ironic sportswear were the other popular choices. Livia, Alexa and Bonnie had made a solid effort, but Watered-Down Club Kid was a hard look to get right. Bonnie, in fishnets and a sleeveless men's shirt held together by one button and a safety pin, was probably doing best out of the three. Yu-jin, having begged out of the wedding party on the basis that she was sick, had now gone on holiday to Naples to make video art in the catacombs and got lost there for several hours before the guide found her. It made the international news and her friend had been livid.

ArteMs had been established by Oxford grads and was one of two rival lesbian club nights that ran every few months in East London. The Cambridge version was called Merkin and played slightly more R&B. Exactly the same crowd of women went to both nights, except for their respective DJs, who maintained a bitter and lengthy feud nobody could quite get to the bottom of. Most of the regulars had been children the first time plastic chokers were trendy, but increasing numbers of even younger women were now filtering through. They looked lustrous and untouched, like butterflies with the bloom still on them. They held no appeal for Livia.

The queue for the bar was four deep and Red Stripes cost a fiver per can, but at least the shots were on offer. They did two each and fought back through the crowd. Livia was gazing at a tall, sullen-looking girl with a white streak in her hair. Alexa leant over and said, 'I've been there and I can tell you that's a bad idea.' Livia had not been scoping out the girl in earnest. As she spent more time with Belle, she'd begun to recognise the comforting sensation of her will retreating, bundling itself up into the protective constriction of another woman's desires, it almost didn't matter whose.

The DJs had already played '212' and 'Anaconda', so the playlist could only go downhill from that point on. After many long years of service, 'Only Girl (In the World)' had finally been retired. When Alexa mimed holding a cigarette to her lips, they swaddled their tinnies in the deepest folds of their jackets to protect them from the zealotry of the door bitches and headed upstairs for the smoking area.

Girls were clustered in groups of three or four, hunched over and scowling despite the late summer heat. Although the three of them had promised before they went out that this time they really would make more effort to mingle, they found a corner and listened as Alexa began to tell them about her latest conquest, who was apparently very flexible and very discreet but who Alexa suspected was leaving her creepy voicemails of someone laughing from a blocked number. Since Alexa did not date girls, she could be absolutely brazen in her pursuit of them – no romantic pride depended on the success of the encounter. She blew two plumes of smoke out through her nose before asking Livia:

'And how is your mysterious older woman?'

'She's living up to expectations. I'm being taken to the opera next week.'

Livia was already planning the ingratiating things she would say, the precise tone of her laughter and the expression she would wear as she got on her knees. The sting of Belle's palm against her cheek.

'Wait, how much older is this woman than you?' Bonnie's face was gleaming with sweat which caught the light as the doors to the club swung open again, spewing more women onto the tiny terrace. She passed a hand over her forehead, and two of the best-looking girls in the neighbouring group looked approvingly at her abundantly hirsute pits.

'You know, I'm not really sure how old Belle is. At first, I thought she was only ten years older than me, but she keeps talking about the work she did in Russia in the eighties, so that can't be right. I mean, however old she is, she's very well preserved.'

Alexa nodded approvingly. 'Quite right, age is just a number.'

'Well, yes and no. Look at some of the girls in here, I'm pretty sure they haven't even heard of Section 28. How am I meant to relate to someone whose experience hasn't been saturated in shame?'

Alexa smiled, stroked Livia's collarbone and said, 'Please look after yourself. It's supposed to be fun, you know.' Unspoken between them was the night that one of Livia's requests had resulted in Alexa taking her to A&E for stitches.

Bonnie lit a new cigarette with her old one and ground the stub out against the wall. She asked, 'It's getting a little tired, isn't it, you doing the same thing over and over again? You're going to get hurt.'

'But it isn't the same thing, this one likes me far more than I like her. She's bought a flat in Shoreditch and wants me to live in it, supposedly so it won't sit empty while she's away in Leipzig.'

171

Livia couldn't help smirking at Bonnie's revolted face before she said, 'You really think we're going to find anyone in here? You wouldn't rather be literally anywhere else, if you had anywhere to go that wasn't full of straight people?'

'You're going to be a kept woman. In this day and age.'

'I've never been anything but a kept woman. Nor have you, for that matter.'

Bonnie turned away and started talking to Alexa about her quest to work out who had been stealing the props from *Peer Gynt*. They kept going missing, and while Bonnie initially guessed it was a prank on James's part, James had since been knocked off his bicycle by a lorry, while the disappearances continued. Alexa made sympathetic noises while scoping out a curvy brunette girl in a halter top. Livia finished her beer, then crushed the can into a shiny silver disc under her foot and set off back towards the doors alone.

VII.

Belle opened the door to their box and ushered Livia into the anteroom, as the orchestra began again after the interval, the sound of violins rising sinuously above the swelling overture. Livia was carrying a metal bucket with the remaining half of their champagne. Belle seized the bucket from her hands and pressed Livia back into the narrow wall with a long kiss, out of sight of the opposite box. She could already hear Faust's rival Siebel trilling onstage about his love for Marguerite. Belle put her hands round Livia's throat and squeezed, studying her face intently then keeping her grip tight for a few beats after Livia tried to tap out.

'Not so full of bravado now, but you can bear more than you think.'

She fussed over Livia's hair, arranging the curls to hide any pink marks, then, tugging up the neckline of the green silk shift she'd picked out for her that afternoon, said, 'Good girl. You scrub up very well indeed.'

Livia found her eyes drawn to the bucket on the shelf, where she could see a distorted reflection of her dress, but nothing of Belle's red one. She simply wasn't there. Noticing the direction of her gaze, Belle reached into the bucket for a lump of ice, posted it down the front of Livia's dress and pushed Livia out towards their seats, hissing in her ear, 'Stay still and don't embarrass me.'

Marguerite twirled about the stage, entranced first by Siebel's bouquet and then by the jewels placed there for her by Mephistopheles. Livia sat with her back poker straight as the ice melted enough to unstick from her skin. She hoped the water wouldn't pool in her skirts and leave a stain, while Belle's hand gripped her knee. She kept it there throughout the duel scene and Marguerite's thwarted attempts to reach the Cathedral, then took Livia's hand as Marguerite resigned herself to the hangman's noose, bending back her pinky finger to breaking point without taking her eyes off the stage. Marguerite's frenzied refusal of Faust at the last moment reverberated in Livia's chest and thrilled her with its repudiation. As he sank, despairing, into the earth, accompanied by the gloating of a heavenly choir, she came, electrified with dread and frustrated propriety. Just before the applause, Belle let go and said, 'Don't answer immediately, but I have a proposal that might interest you.'

VIII.

The bells of Paris were ringing nine and Livia had all of ten minutes to fold away the bed and get ready to help open the shop. She rolled over and almost out of the tiny rickety camp bed she had been sleeping on, which smelt distinctly of male sweat. Livia was in the poetry section again, not having been able to wangle a bed in the studio flat upstairs. Perhaps the sweat was Roland's, since it was through his recommendation that she'd secured her place here. He'd often said that being too preoccupied with cleanliness was tragic, though given that his basement flat had recently been flooded with filth after a storm it remained to be seen how strongly he would continue to obey this maxim. Livia was more than a week into her stay, but she was still surprised to wake every morning and find herself extracted from muggy, doomed London, whose streets she walked continually in her dreams, accompanied by a little black dog.

She and the two young Swedes who had monopolised the studio, plus the taciturn Argentinian boy who slept in Art Reference, folded back the shutters of the shop windows, rearranged the books on the table displays and lugged the wheeled shelves outside onto the cobbles. After this she felt about ready to go back to bed, but as her bed was stashed under a divan where young Americans were now sitting reading the best-known bits of Hemingway to each other, she sloped off to the little park next to the shop and lit up a cigarette.

As she'd intended to do every day since she'd arrived, she unlocked her phone, ready to message Belle her final acquiescence. She'd been sent pictures of the flat: well lit, without much in the way of decor. No hints of Belle's taste. She had promised Livia could fit it out to her own requirements, since she would be the one to spend most time there.

Instead, Livia took a picture of the boxy Greek church at the edge of the park and posted it online. Not half an hour later she felt her phone buzz against the zinc counter where she was drinking strong, overpriced coffee and turned it face up to see a message from Annie. Her body felt hollow, like all her organs had been whisked away.

'Don't know what you're doing here but would be good to see you. You free for a drink in the Marais this evening?'

It was still warm and light when she got there and Annie had bought them a carafe of white wine, perspiring gently onto the tablecloth. She was overcome by a rush of familiar affection, unkillable after all this time, and watched Annie turning the empty glass around and around in her hands. The same hands which had violated her and written her love letters (subsequently burnt) and had rebuilt an entire life away from London after Annie came out and was rejected by her mother for being an unrepentant sinner. The same hands which earnt Annie a living, though not much of one, as a baker's apprentice and which were visibly trembling so much that Livia feared she would drop the glass and break it.

While she was waiting for Annie to regain her composure, she couldn't help but circle back to the unwelcome memory. It gained more details each time. The storm had wailed so loud that from inside their tightly curtained room, Livia felt she could almost see through the walls to watch the air turning in great loops and tunnels over the lake. She was curled over with her back to Annie, who was also crying. They had been fighting because Annie had insisted Livia's friends' decision to play Scrabble in Latin was a deliberate choice to exclude her. Livia had lost her temper at this interpretation. When Annie heard the howling, she'd laughed nervously and asked what the noise was, though Livia wasn't talking to her. On being told that it was just the wind blowing over the moors, she said:

'I didn't ask for any of this, I'm a city girl you know.'

Livia had pointed out she was from London too and hadn't understood that Annie was alluding to the differences between them.

Livia's Scottish surname came from the architect who had designed Edinburgh New Town, while Annie's Scottish surname came from the family who had owned her family and whose castle still stood on the Borders. Annie had once shown her a picture of it online. All Livia had thought to say was that she hoped the cost of keeping the roof up would ruin them.

Annie pointed at the tight silver necklace Livia was wearing, with one fat black pearl strung through its centre, gleaming pink and green in the last of the light.

'You're seeing someone?'

'Sort of. She wants a lot from me, and I don't know if I can do it.'

Annie filled Livia's glass, though her wrist was shaking. By the time she pulled away, it was almost too full to drink. A waiter stood poised nearby with a cloth and an expression of distaste. Livia prayed he would not get involved.

'That doesn't sound so good. You're usually pretty certain what you want.'

Livia drew back.

'No, you're usually pretty certain what I want.'

She considered saying more, how there were certain acts she no longer enjoyed and had only just remembered why, how she still had to go in that room sometimes and sleep there. How furious she was with Annie for making her a victim when that wasn't how she saw herself.

Annie looked down and breathed heavily for a few moments, wheezing like she might break out into sobs.

Livia said none of these things, it seemed spiteful and pointless to keep hammering home Annie's guilt.

'I'm so sorry . . . I was trying to feel close to you, but I should never have done it, I know that.' Annie hunched over and hugged her knees, taking gulps of wine. She looked very tired and the waiter was still staring at her as if she ought not to be there.

Livia felt in every sinew the urge to comfort Annie, to come round and embrace her and say it hadn't been so bad. She fought it and sat there in silence, uncertain of what to do.

Then Annie pushed back her chair, making a scraping sound on the pavement and stood up. She pulled out her rucksack from beneath her feet and dumped it on the table. Livia could see that the red leather had cracked apart down the centre and been sutured back together with a thick black shoelace, now going fuzzy. Annie reached inside the bag and searched around, spreading papers and cables and pots of half-used lip balm over the tablecloth.

'I have something for you. I should have done this years ago.'

Annie pushed a small green velvet box towards her. Livia thought for one mad moment that there might be a ring inside, then wondered, not without regret, if there could ever have been a world in which she would have accepted.

After Annie had rushed through her goodbyes and left, Livia took off the black pearl from around her neck and put it into the box, beside the ribbon.

It wasn't even dark yet and she'd heard there was a friendly little place not far from there, where all manner of things were permitted.

Saplings

If I had known, Tam Lin, she said,
You would have always been alone
For I'd have cut out your mortal heart
And put in a heart of stone

The fields were not yet at full ripeness, but already they brimmed with wheat. Kites circled above, occasionally swooping to catch unseen prey. The hedgerows spilled over themselves, spreading pink and white flowers into pastureland. Finally, I was on my way to Rowan. The stop-start motion of the old train did not prevent me sinking into vague dreams of running my fingers through her hair and biting her lips – so full and red and out of my mouth for far too long. The moment she had called to invite me, I'd bought a ticket and cancelled all my plans. If she wanted to see me again, I would be there, my tattered dignity could not prevent it. Only slow trains went from London, this one had stopped at ten or twelve slate-roofed stations on the way, without a soul to be seen waiting at any of them and no one disembarking. I had been wrestling with my fears since her abrupt departure a month before, but the steady whoosh along the tracks, drawing us ever closer, lulled me and allowed me to set them down a while.

She was standing outside the station, leaning against her old motorbike and peering down the lane into the distance. I waited for her to notice I'd arrived, savouring the chance to look at her before her gaze could turn back on me, and perhaps find me lacking. That was my checked shirt, left at her flat with vague assurances I could come back to claim it, before she got too sick to see anyone. Although she'd told me she no longer felt quite safe here, she was standing straight again and the feverish sheen on her skin had gone.

Everything I could say caught in my throat at once, but I must have made some sound, since she turned and gave me a calm half-smile. She said, 'My father's back, he arrived last night. He didn't say a word to me or even knock – I only heard him because I was awake. He's in Lesser Sarsen now, buying cheese, I imagine.'

I held myself rigid, rather than stepping forward to embrace her, as my pleasant daydreams of long baths and sunbathing together on the lawn drained away. I had hoped that she would feel more able to talk to me openly at her home, but now he would be here too. She'd told me he would gone for a fortnight. The only thing her father wanted was a son and he'd never accepted she couldn't be that for him. Henry still insisted on treating her as if she were a boy even after she had gathered all her courage to tell him that she wasn't one. He refused to acknowledge that his wish had not been granted.

I said, 'You could have called to tell me that. Is everything alright?'

She slid her phone out of her back pocket and showed me the screen. Not a single bar.

'The storm last winter took out three telephone poles and no one's come to fix them. I'm not convinced that anyone is going to, they enjoy their peace and quiet. I had to ride up to the Old Fort just to ask you down here.'

'I'm sorry, I hadn't realised it was that bad.'

I let myself wrap my arms around her at last, breathing in her familiar floral perfume and unexpected notes of fresh earth. Perhaps a full retreat from the world was what she'd needed. The last few times we'd seen each other, she had only asked questions about my life and deflected every inquiry I made. She kept saying she had something urgent to research and would be free to spend more time with me soon. I'd had to keep waking her because she was whimpering in her sleep. Sometimes she said my name, but when I told her this, she could never remember why. I longed to help her, if only she would let me.

Rowan took my rucksack and started securing it to the pillion with a length of chain as I put on the spare helmet. I got on behind her, inching in close and darting a kiss to the soft skin at the back of her neck. I couldn't see anyone around us, but the force of my desire was so strong that often I found myself behaving in an exaggeratedly chaste fashion because to acknowledge even a fraction of it felt impossible when I knew nothing of our surroundings. Letting me settle around her, she adjusted my hands on her waist, giving one a squeeze, before she kicked the bike into life.

'Lean with me when I take a turn and don't let go. These country roads, you never know who's coming round the bend.'

We shot away from the station in a cloud of grit and ochre dust, every rock in the road sending jolts through my spine as I gloried in the onward motion. Past a shuttered post office and a church, with its great yew tree looming and packed gravestones pressed right up against the wall. Past mud-spattered jeeps and a miserable-looking child on a piebald pony. A woman dressed in dull green hunting clothes trudging down a lane. Soon we were gloriously alone, rushing past fields of cows and down steep hills, just us and the world unfurling. For the last moments of the downward swoop we would lift off the ground entirely, in flight. I wished we could be like this forever, nestled close and moving weightlessly as one, with no danger of her leaving me behind. Every verge was crowded with foxgloves and campion, and I thought I could see primroses in the shady spots, but the whistling air around us was so loud I couldn't ask.

After the sign for the Old Fort, we turned off down the drive into the forest towards Carterhaugh. She'd told me that parts of it threatened to engulf the house, her father had stopped bothering to cut it back after her mother disappeared. It was tall and thick around us now, with snippets of birdsong audible on the breeze as we blasted through.

I had seen pictures of her with her house in the background before, though not many, as I didn't want to break Rowan's trust by seeking out pictures of her before the age of eighteen, when she'd first begun to accept she was trans. The house was made of darker stone than I'd imagined and looked bulkier, as if hunched over something precious, shielding it from the hills around.

'You need to grip less tightly, there were points back there it felt like you were trying to pull my insides out.'

'Sorry, I got scared that if I held you any looser you'd leave me in the dust.' She pulled off her helmet, hair darkened with perspiration, and I felt the unfairness all over again. She hadn't even warned me she was leaving – I had showed up to the flat to give her an early twenty-first birthday present and waited outside for so long that a neighbour had to tell me he'd seen her with a suitcase. I tried to smooth over my hurt, afraid that it would show through as resentment. Surely if she had asked me here, it was because she wanted to mend things between us? I would give everything I had, if she would tell me what she needed.

On my way up to the door, my foot caught against something and I tripped. A little blue bowl of milk went skittering across the flagstones, teetered perilously for a moment and righted itself, unbroken, while its contents soaked into the moss.

'Do you have a cat?'

'It's a local superstition, apparently the good folk like it. Kay must have been here, for the rabbits.'

'That raises more questions than it answers.'

Rowan pushed open the heavy double doors. 'I'll explain later, I imagine you'll want to shower before this evening.'

'Are you coming too?'

'I had one this morning.'

I felt a little pang of the usual sadness, followed by its accompanying guilt. Often she could hardly stand to be unclothed with me, let alone touched. She did not seem to believe my answers when she asked if I could really desire her as she was. Day by day the planes of her lovely face softened, her scent shifted, and she was often overcome by tears at small gestures, like my bringing a bottle of her favourite cordial. I had wanted her when I first met her and I wanted her still, I would go on wanting her no matter how much she did or did not change.

I followed her quietly through the house. It was dim and cool, with threadbare carpets laid out over curving stones and squat velvet-covered sofas. And over everything, a fine layer of dust. Even in spring, it smelt of mildew and stale air. I kept stopping to admire the house's many treasures: a pale green celadon bowl with a vein of gold running through it; a vitrine of tiny flint arrowheads suspended on a red felt backing with silver pins, each resting in their own alcoves; a dark wooden stick carved with the faces of birds and men leant in the corner of the hall.

Peering into one room, I saw the walls were hung with threadbare tapestries showing faded scenes of a huntsman out riding in a forest, presented with a swaddled baby by a hooded figure in an elegant flowing cloak, with a crown of leaves and blooming flowers on its head. On the next wall, the huntsman with his wife and child, now grown knee-high, were confronted by the hooded figure, surrounded by his silver-clad retinue who menaced them with spears and bows. In the third tapestry, the figure was dragging away the wife on a chain, while the wife's face was straining back to see her child. Turning to look at the final panel, which hung over the double doors, I saw the figure on a palanquin, watching from under its hood with a posture that somehow conveyed lively amusement as the wife was consumed by a lake of flames, surrounded by grey standing stones.

Rowan saw I'd stopped and called me to hurry on upstairs. The guest room was white-walled and anonymous, apart from an iron bedstead and some framed etchings of herbs. She washed her hands in the sink of the bathroom next door as I undressed. I saw her watching closely in the mirror, though she did not come to me.

'Rowan, what's wrong? Have I done something to upset you?'

'I wish you'd stop asking me that. I was exhausted and I needed to be alone for a while.'

My face must have fallen, because she crossed the room and put her arms around me, kissing the top of my head and drawing me close.

'Trust me, it will all be OK, you're here now.' She gently pressed her lips to mine.

Just being near her was enough to soothe me. It had been that way since the night we met, when she'd seen me standing alone at a party, deliberating over whether I should just turn and leave. She'd beckoned me over to sit with her and asked whether I wanted to hear a story. I said that I did. Not far from where she had grown up, there was a stone circle. It wasn't large or historically significant and so not many people cared about it except for the locals, who called it the Old Fort. Every time someone counted the stones, they got a different number. Everyone but her.

'Surely that settled it, then?'

'We used to drink in that field and my friends would often make a game of counting. I could tell I was annoying them. There wasn't much else to do and we were very bored. Eventually I began to lie and said different numbers. Then I told them I'd forgotten the number I'd originally counted.'

'So how many are there?'

Rowan had just laughed and unlocked her phone, saying that maybe she'd tell me one day, but before I left the party there was another number she wanted to know.

By the time her father came back, we were downstairs drinking pink gin with orange halves and doing the crossword. I'd looked for pictures of her mother under the pretext of opening the window in the sitting room to let through a breeze, but spotted none. The catch was painted over. She had run away when Rowan was seven without leaving so much as a note. Rowan's father had no one else but her.

Henry had been beautiful once, before the weather got to him. A long, pale face with sprigs of burst veins about the nose and cheeks. His sharp blue eyes took in my half-shaved head, shapeless black cotton dress and bare feet resting on a little inlaid stool in one disapproving sweep.

'I wondered whose big boots those were by the door. How'd you do?'

I got up to shake his hand, which he deflected, moving in for a kiss on the cheek. Truly, one of the old school, then.

'Pleased to meet you. Your house is lovely, I always wanted to see where Rowan grew up.'

'Well, it's a bit of a state at the moment, as you might have noticed.'

Rowan set about pouring some of the pink gin for her father, which he ignored, making his way to the drinks cabinet and extracting a bottle of Hendrick's along with a fresh glass.

He said, 'Our last housekeeper Sarah had a heart attack seven years ago and we've not been able to find anyone else worth keeping on since then. Kay still does a bit for the garden, but only when she feels like coming by.'

I said, 'I suppose she must have lots of people to see with all this greenery. I thought the landscape on my way here was wonderful.'

After a period of deliberation, Henry accepted an orange segment and sat opposite us.

'It does have that effect on some people, especially at this time of year. Coming back through Ridlington, I noticed those crusties have set up camp in the far field again, near the Old Fort. It's disgraceful. I was in the forest a couple of weeks ago and found a couple of them wearing antlers and prancing about. On my land. They insisted the king of the fairies and his court would bless them for it and they had right of way because of the footpath.'

I burst out laughing at the image, and Rowan laughed with me, which seemed to mollify him a little. He shifted towards us in his chair.

'I'm afraid it's a kitchen supper tonight, just cold cuts. I haven't had a moment to make anything – unless you have?' He turned to face me and waited.

I tried not to let any suggestion of the insult he had offered both of us cross my face.

'I'm afraid I didn't know where anything was and didn't like to ransack someone else's kitchen without permission.'

'I'd have thought it was fairly clear where everything is. You can cook, can't you? Someone's clearly been feeding Rowan.'

Henry pinched her upper arm and chuckled. 'I ought to send you out to chop some logs, get those muscles working again. Don't you want to impress her?' He paused. 'You *are* a her, aren't you? I can't keep up with all of Rowan's notions.'

I emptied any remaining warmth from my voice. 'Yes, that is an accurate way to refer to both me and Rowan.' People had only started questioning me when they knew about her and it made me uncertain in turn. What if I too could be more than I'd been allowed to imagine?

'What do your parents think of your hair? It's very bold, isn't it?'

190

I said airily, 'I wouldn't know, I haven't seen them in a while.' I let the implicit threat dangle. *If I can do it, so can she.*

Rowan said, 'I'm hungry, can we go through?' By then she had drained her glass, but I couldn't catch her eye. She had never told me he'd behave like this, though I suppose I should have guessed.

Supper consisted of old cabbage, hard-boiled potatoes from the fridge and green beans in a sludgy clear sauce. I cut into a chicken thigh, only to find that it was still pink. Fortunately, Henry had also provided us with cloth napkins. I talked a lot about the most inoffensive nothings I could think of, which became easier the more dry white wine I consumed. Normally Rowan had a story or a comment for every occasion, but tonight her conversation was vague agreement and disavowal. At the end of the meal, I insisted on helping to clear away the plates, which allowed me the chance to throw out the contents of my bulging napkin. The smell emanating from the sink was so bad that I nearly threw up the few beans and lone potato I had managed. Rowan wouldn't let me help any more than I already had, so I watched her wipe down every piece of pearl-handled cutlery with a damp cloth, taking care to clean each individual tine. Her father gestured towards the guest bedroom she'd shown me and told her to fetch 'whatever I had come with'.

I'd hoped I could sneak back down to Rowan, or at least to the kitchen, to cobble together something from the fabled Lesser Sarsen cheese, but having lain down on the sagging mattress, I found I could not get back up, even to remove my clothes. The wine lay hot and heavy on me like a fever and several times I was half woken by dreams that there was a commotion going on around the bed, as if arrangements were being made that required a great deal of bustling back and forth and much conversation in low voices I could never quite catch. The blankets were prickly and for a long time I couldn't get comfortable enough to completely drift off.

I woke sweaty and bedraggled, much too late after noon to show my face in the kitchen. This time I made it down to her bedroom, though I found she'd already gone. A pile of battered, cloth-bound books with intricate circular symbols embossed on the spines sat stacked on the table by her bed. I opened the topmost volume at the place marked by its ribbon to read the beginning of a chapter headed 'Teinds & Tithes: How Not to Pay', but couldn't make any sense of the text and my head ached from broken sleep. She had always liked old things, she'd nailed a battered horseshoe over the door to her flat and given me an antique glass bottle full of fragrant rosemary to sit on my windowsill. Looking in the mirror, I could see that with all the tossing and turning, my hair had worked itself into knots and tangles that would become impossible to undo if I slept on them another night. I let myself into Rowan's bathroom to borrow conditioner and a comb, as it would take more than the miniature bottle I had brought to fix the chaos. The whole room was nautical-themed, with six different tiny ships in bottles and an old wooden steering wheel hanging over the tub. She'd told me that she longed to learn to sail, but her father had forbidden it. This must have been his version of compromise. I ran the tap and soaked as I forced the comb through my hair, trying not to pull more of it out at the roots than could be helped and crying, first from the pain and then for the many lonely evenings she had spent in here, a long way inland but dreaming up a life of adventure and escape from Carterhaugh. Rowan loved to tell me stories about famous mutinies and lethal explosions at sea, preferring this to the minutiae of her week or her hopes for the future.

Drying my eyes and my detangled hair, I went to find my boots. I looked through the long window and saw her bike wasn't where she'd left it. For one moment, I had the urge to grab my bag and simply walk out, back to the station without a word. Perhaps she was testing me, to see if I would abandon her like her mother. Instead I settled on a walk to pass the time. The sun was hot, but I wasn't long out of the shade. I headed in as fast as I could, hoping to avoid engaging in any further pleasantries with Henry if he was at large. As the trees grew thicker, I passed an old well, overgrown with ivy and missing its cover, so one could peer straight down into the darkness at the bottom. I took a winding route, little caring where my feet led me. Young ferns unfurled among the rocks and brambles caught at my hem. The scent of late bluebells mingled with wild garlic shoots crushed underfoot. The birds were quiet here. My calves had started to ache from walking on uneven ground and I sat beneath an old ash tree. In a sunlit patch of grass nearby, I saw a strange flower, its petals drooping like a snowdrop, but much larger, chequered purple and white. It was so delicate and bold at the same time, I was determined to bring it back for Rowan. As I leant out to pluck it, I heard a low voice say:

'I wouldn't do that if I were you.'

Emerging from the trees, I saw the same woman I'd spotted in the lane, with two dead rabbits hanging over one shoulder. She walked into the clearing and bent down into a squat next to me.

'They're very rare. It's bad luck to take them.' She lifted the flower's head with the tip of a finger, as if examining it for damage.

'You must be Kay.'

She looked at me sharply. She had even features and a small, pointed chin. One eye was filmed over, almost white. Up close she looked younger than I had assumed, though I couldn't place her age. Rowan said Kay was the only person who'd been kind when she came out.

'Is this something to do with the bowl of milk Rowan was talking about?'

'You shouldn't be here, it's not safe.'

'If you're laying traps, can't you just tell me which parts to avoid?'

She swatted a fly that was trying to settle on one of the rabbits and said again, 'You shouldn't be here.'

I rolled my eyes. 'Well help me find a flower I can take back to the house and I'll go away.'

She thought for a minute, brow furrowed, then took my wrist and led me a little way on. Her hands were rough and warm. I allowed myself to wonder how they might feel around my hips.

We reached a tree laden with white blossoms and I reached out carefully to break off a thorny branch. I felt her hand close over mine, adding her weight to break it off. I shrieked as long spikes pierced the flesh of my palm. She picked up the branch and stood watching as I put my hand to my mouth to try and suck out any dirt that might have been left in the wounds. Without apologising, she put the branch into my unpunctured hand. It was heavier than I'd anticipated and some of the white flowers were now speckled with my blood. A patch of ground underneath was stained where I had spat out the bitter mess. She looked at me expectantly and then at the flowers I held.

'Off you go, the house is in that direction.'

My hand throbbed and my stomach turned and twisted with hunger. I began to hurry, feeling bad that I had clearly disappointed her in some way. I couldn't think how to describe the encounter without getting her in trouble with Henry, so I resolved not to mention it.

I'd been gone longer than I thought. Rowan was dozing in a lawn chair outside the house, in the last of the late evening sun, hair twisted into one long braid that lay over her shoulder. I woke her with a kiss on the forehead and presented her with the branch.

'Be careful, it's very sharp.'

195

'They're beautiful.' Her face took on the cast it did when she was trying not to cry.

'Like you. Where were you this afternoon?'

'I went for a spin on the bike.'

'Where did you ride to?'

'Just in a circuit, here and back.'

I gave up and plucked a few flowers from the branch with my good hand, twisting them into the end of her braid, which seemed to cheer her a little.

'Come in for supper, we're eating early and I think you'll enjoy what my father has prepared.'

Rowan rose from the chair and beckoned me toward her, meeting my kiss with passion when I took her in my arms. We held each other for a long moment, so tightly that I lost my breath. I tried to relax into the embrace, hoping that the thudding of her heart against my chest would slow a little, but it didn't. She drew back and opened her mouth to speak, before she looked behind her and seemed to think better of it.

'Just remember that I love you very much,' she said. Then she took my hand and led me to the dark green dining room, at the far end of the house from the terrace, where the trees tapped against the French windows, not looking back. Her father was still laying the table as we walked in, pouring red wine into a thick glass decanter and adjusting the plates of food to set each one off to best effect. Harsh acid crept up from my belly to my throat and my mouth watered. Glistening meats were laid out on a china plate, while cheeses sweated softly on a board nearby. Whole globe artichokes sat next to bowls of sautéed wild mushrooms in pools of butter and handfuls of fresh cress. The scent of potted shrimp rose above the tang of freshly baked bread. Here were the first strawberries of the year and a bowl of sugar to dip them into. I hadn't even sat down and I could hardly stop myself from tearing in without regard for anyone else.

'I see you went exploring today. You might at least have washed your face before coming in.' Henry swayed a little in his chair, cheeks ruddy with wine and sun.

'There was no one around to tell me when I would be needed.'

'Did no one ever teach you that it's rude for young ladies to lie in bed while everyone else is up and going about their day?' Rowan looked even more uncomfortable than she had the night before. Why did she let him talk to me like this? I watched her comb her fingers through the hair at the end of her braid, frantically seeking out small tangles to pry them apart.

I said that I was sorry and reached out for the nearest dishes to serve myself, not caring what was in them.

'I accept your apology. Now please let's enjoy the meal.' He sat and watched me intently, his own fork still on the table. Rowan reached for a serving spoon, as if to make up a plate for me, but then sat back abruptly. Not sure what to do but eat, I took a little of everything and broke off a hunk of bread, feeling the flour dust my fingertips, then ran it through a thick sauce, fragrant with lamb and juniper.

'Don't!' Rowan jumped out of her chair and reached across, knocking my plate onto the floor where it broke.

'What is WRONG with you?' I grabbed a napkin and started cleaning the spattered food off my face and chest.

She said weakly, 'Please don't. Don't eat any of it.' I wasn't sure why she looked so frightened, hands pressed flat pushing at the edge of the table like she was about to spring up again. Then Henry rose and slowly came to stand behind her. Suddenly, he grabbed her by the collar and pulled Rowan to her feet, screaming 'Stupid! Fucking! Idiot!' as he jerked her back and forth like a ragdoll. Raising his hand high, he slapped Rowan full in the face, letting her reel back before he caught her again to pull her close as he hissed, 'Did you have a better plan? You're weeks overdue already.'

She whimpered, 'I can't let you do this to her.'

I sat, hot stew congealing in my lap, rooted to my chair.

White-knuckled hand still tight around Rowan's collar, he said, 'You have to, you know full well what happens to you if you don't.'

'I don't care, you know this isn't right.'

My voice came back. 'What's in the food?'

Henry carried on. 'You're so weak, it makes me sick. You know what I've had to do just to keep you alive this long, my son, and it's time to pay the tithe again. You want me to give up now, for that? She isn't worth saving, you could find another, better girl in days.' He jerked her head to make her look at me, then said, almost laughing, 'You'd really throw away your mother's sacrifice, and Sarah's, just because you found someone deluded enough to play dress-up with you?'

As if waking from a trance, Rowan sprang back, pulling free from his grip. Then she struck him hard in the jaw. Henry clutched his cheek and tried to say something else, but before he could get the words out, she hit him again in the head. He fell face down on the carpet and lay there, crumpled. Breathing, but out cold.

'I never wanted it to come to this.' Rowan was panting and shaking, looking at her open hand in disbelief.

She knelt and pulled her father's lumpen body over onto his side.

'I think I've found a way to break the curse, but I'm going to need your help.'

My mind spun and churned like a river rising to burst its banks. I shouted, 'You left me. You left London without a single word and now I find out he was going to poison me or drug me or something.'

Still on her knees, Rowan turned to face me. 'Just do this one last thing, I'm begging you. Then you can leave me if you want, I won't blame you.'

I thought back to the time I turned my ankle so badly I couldn't walk and Rowan had come to stay for weeks, making strange poultices of herbs and mud to bring down the swelling and fetching me things before I could even think to ask. She had taken my pain seriously, more so than any of my friends. We had been close then, closer than I'd been with anyone before. And yet, I had not realised the extent of the terror Henry had instilled in her, nor what it would cost her to defy him.

'What do you need?'

'When you were out walking today, did you see a ruined well?'

I nodded.

'Count down from a hundred, then go out to the forest and wait there. When you see me, grab onto me for as long as you can bear it, but when it's time to let go, you have to trust me. Don't keep holding on.'

Rowan jumped up and seized a little bronze-coloured key from its place on the sideboard, then rushed over to the French window and forced it open.

'I don't understand!'

'They will try to use your fears against you, please don't forget my real face.'

She was already one foot out the door, face turned toward the forest.

'I must hurry, don't follow me!'

Ignoring Henry on the floor, I laid my forehead on the cool, dark wood of the table and counted, heart pounding in my chest, full of confusion and dread.

I reached zero and ran into the cold night, stumbling on the uneven ground, although the moon was full and bright. The wind was up and it blew into my eyes, the trees whispered and swayed. Brambles caught at my clothes and nettles scratched my bare legs. The strap broke on one of my shoes so I cast them off and kept running, dead leaves crunching underfoot and sharp twigs piercing my soles. I was unsure of my direction, searching for the shaft of light that would indicate the clearing. Several times I thought I spotted it, but every time I drew close it was just more forest with a gap in the boughs above. A pinprick of flame appeared that danced and floated on the air. All around me more little fires winked into life, weaving dizzily between the trees, snuffing out and reigniting, sometimes dropping onto piles of dead leaves and burning for a while. I wheeled about trying to avoid them, terrified that one would brush my dress or become tangled in my hair. I ran in circles, hopeless of ever finding the well. Turning back to pick another direction at random, blind with fear. Still running into the night without any sense of where I was until suddenly I reached the well.

But the clearing wasn't empty. There, in the moonlight, walked a strange procession clad in hooded silver robes carrying spears decked with blossoms, a great throng singing in low voices, who trod with steps so light they barely seemed to touch the ground. None of them turned to look at me.

Legs shaking, I stepped out and stood in the way to make them halt. For a moment I thought they might turn their weapons on me, or just trample me underfoot, but they stopped. A tall figure stepped forward while the others drew back.

The woods were still and as I looked closer in the halflight I saw the figure's robe was moving not with the breeze but because it was made of spiderwebs, rivulets of dew, dead leaves and insects, and all this living matter flowed down in waves from two curved horns above the hood that nearly touched at their tips like a diadem. It was constantly decaying and falling away and creating itself anew. The cowl of the hood hung too low for me to see a face within.

A high voice spoke, with laughter in it. 'Whatever can you hope to gain by disturbing us, tonight of all nights?'

'Where is Rowan?' I tried not to tremble.

He sounded unsurprised. 'Which one do you mean?'

'She said she would be here.' I tried to pick her out among the figures. The singing intensified, a low and wordless melody that sounded strangely familiar.

'I'll be generous, if you can recognise her. Guess wrong and she burns.'

I scanned the crowd, but they were all the same. The robes glittered and rippled too much for me to make out any shapes underneath. Towards the back of the shimmering horde, I spotted a silver hood with an auburn plait escaping from it, and at the end of that, one little white flower. I pointed.

'That one!'

Two of the others shoved Rowan roughly out of the formation towards me. Surely, it could not be so easy to demand her back and be gratified, or Henry would have done this years ago. It seemed he had visited the court often enough to know something of its ways.

The shrouded king asked, 'Aren't you going to say anything? I didn't have to give her to you. She's ours to burn, we found her first.'

'How do I know it's not a trick?' I asked him.

The voice said, wearily, 'Your kind are so ungrateful, always certain that if you don't get exactly what you hoped for, then we must have cheated. Henry didn't listen to me. But you have paid with your own heart's blood, no substitutes or deluded victims . . . now let's see if you can keep her. We'll find someone else to sate Hell for a little while.'

The procession was already sweeping away towards the Old Fort as I lunged for Rowan.

We wrestled together on the hard ground, as far from the procession as I could roll us. Her silver robe crumbled into nothing, caking us both with dust and twigs. My hands drew tight around her wrists as she struggled to throw me off and rejoin them, eyes wide and unseeing. Then her skin grew slick and I found that instead of Rowan I was grappling with a giant snake, patterned amber coils winding tight around me, choking the air out of my lungs. I writhed in disgust and fright, but kept my arms locked around her. He must have known I had always been terrified of serpents. She swelled out into a bear, bellowing hot breath in my face and snapping dangerously close with giant teeth. I shoved her coarse-furred back against the wall of the well and dug my heels into the ground, while her claws tore the flesh from my shoulders. Still I held on. It was still her, I'd know her anywhere despite the vicious illusions the shrouded king called forth.

She took on human form again, but this time she had my face, distorted to fit my ugliest, most secret fears of how I must look to her. Screaming incomprehensibly with my voice, she tried to fight me off with a strength that felt like twice my own. All I could do was wrap my arms around her waist and squeeze.

Then she became a stinking cadaver, flopping in my grasp and gushing foul liquid from her mouth. I shrieked and retched while she disintegrated into black mulch, as I was trying to shake her back to life, imploring her to open her eyes.

What was left of Rowan in my hands grew warm and bright, and then white hot, sticking to my hands and scorching them, I feared almost to the bone. I screamed and jerked and watched in horror as she flew out of my hands and rolled over the lip of the well, down into the darkness.

I called and called into the well, but heard no answer.

The sun rose and stayed up for a while and began to set again. Eventually my eyes ran dry. I hoped that if I could stay there long enough, I would dissolve into the earth and perhaps drain down to meet her.

As the evening dew settled over me, I thought I heard a scratching, rustling noise. I sat up, but there was silence. After a long time, it started again. Whatever was coming for me now, I didn't know or care. The noise grew louder. It began to sound more like heaving and gasping. I refused to believe what I was hearing, until I saw Rowan heave herself back over the edge and tumble onto the ground, naked and covered in filth, wheezing from the effort.

She was still whole and still herself and she had come back to me. I took her bleeding hands in my burnt ones and we helped each other to our feet.

Acknowledgements

Perhaps appropriately, *Parallel Hells* took me seven years to write, between the first draft of the first story stirring into life on the screen of my laptop and my wonderful editor Francine Toon declaring it complete and ready to go to copyedit. If that span of time is a teind of my own, I give it gladly and am grateful to emerge mostly unburnt.

If those seven years have taught me anything, it is that however determined one might be, it is nearly impossible for any of us to climb out of the well alone. I have been immensely lucky with the people who have taught, supported and encouraged me along the way. Trying to count them all is a daunting task, and if I have omitted anyone, it is not because you are not loved but rather that your name has been etched into my heart for so long it has become part of the flesh.

In no particular order, I would like to thank my teachers for putting up with my teenage goth histrionics and encouraging me to mainline Chaucer and Webster, my tutors from UCL and Oxford for indulging my love of Medieval and Gothic literature (and my speculations about Njal Thorgeirsson's romantic life), and the Birkbeck MFA course tutors for giving me the push I sorely needed to get on with *Parallel Hells*. I owe special gratitude to Julia Bell for her insightful and generous mentorship, and for making me laugh so often in our tutorials and to Toby Litt for steering the ship during a very difficult year.

I am much indebted to my beloved friends, who read many drafts of the stories, gave me incisive feedback, came to my readings and lifted my spirits when they were low, particularly Hugh Foley, Tristan Rogers, Alexander Gamble, Levi Scott, Rosanna Mallinson, Angharad Monk, Elisa Mozzanica, Ned Carter-Miles, Sophie Ruigrok, Naomi Ishiguro, Ben Noble and the rest of the UCL crew. Thank you to Caroline Batten for her never-endingly delightful queer medieval gossip. Thank you to Donald McDonald and the rest of the Failed Novelists Society for getting me back into writing regularly. Thank you to my MFA classmates for the warmth, solidarity and their unerring ability to spot plot holes. Thank you to Melissa Watkins for the story exchanges and the beautiful music from Strange Eyes. Thank you to Julia Mattison for her manuscript expertise and infectious enthusiasm. Thank you to Geffen Semach for her friendship and sage writing advice. Thank you to Ksenya Blokhina for the zakuski and deep Slavic loyalty. To the lovely Alice Anokhina, who yanked me back out of Hell more times than I can count, thank you so much.

I owe more thanks than I can express to my parents, Robin and Amanda, for filling our house with books, for steadfastly supporting my desire to read and write and for all their generosity, acceptance and love towards me over the course of my life. Thank you to my brother William for the provision of rare memes and longbois. Thank you to my grandmothers and my extended family at large for all their exuberance, eccentricity and sweetness. Thank you to my darling Anat, for coming along towards the end and giving me hope that cruel tales are not the only ones worth telling.

Immense respect and many thanks to Olumide Popoola for founding and running the Futures in the Making and Future is Back projects for LGBTQI+ writers, your vision and fortitude are invaluable.

Thank you to everyone at the *White Review* past and present for giving me my first real break with 'Mute Canticle' when I had no confidence in my writing and for continuing to surprise and delight me.

Many, many thanks to all of the magazines and literary websites which have published my work in earlier versions, listed at the back of this book.

Thank you to my friends and colleagues at Profile and Serpent's Tail, who have taught me so much about literature, the business of art and what it really means to care for books, and to Hannah Westland, Rebecca Gray and Andrew Franklin in particular.

Many thanks to Leyla Çolpan for hir sensitive and thoughtful advice on depicting transfeminine people respectfully, though any remaining infelicities are mine to own.

Thank you to my brilliant agent Matt Turner, for all of his dry wit, dedication and attention to detail and to everyone at Rogers, Coleridge and White – British fiction wouldn't be the same without you.

Thank you to Francine Toon, my wonderful editor – one crepuscular soul always knows another and working on *Parallel Hells* with you has been the greatest treat I could ask for! I'm so lucky to have had your expert eyes on my work. Thank you to Maria Garbutt-Lucero and Louise Court, publicists of dreams, Helen Flood and everyone at Sceptre who has had a hand in the making of this book, even if I have not yet had the pleasure of meeting them - I know all too well how vital and interconnected each step of the publication process is, and I'm so appreciative of everything you've done to make this book not only real but something I can be proud of.

Lastly, thank you to all the LGBTQI+ artists and writers who came before me and came up with me, whose work has sustained and challenged me, and who have made trying to put some of this queer life of ours down on paper seem possible.

Previously Published Stories

The following stories were published in earlier versions elsewhere:

'No Dominion' was published on *Queen Mob's Teahouse*

'raw pork and opium' was published on Storgy.com

'Ingratitude' was performed as the short radio play 'Dateless Night' by Storyectpod.com for their *Secrets* show

'Suckers' was published by theshortstory.co.uk as 'Yucatán' and won a Young Writer's Award

'Unfinished and Unformed' was published in *Determined Hearts: A Frankenstein Anthology* (ed. Jacqueline Dorsey)

'Pretty Rooms' was published in the (sadly now defunct) *Next Review*

'Stay a While' was published on the *Mechanics' Institute Review* website